Cheating Justice

A novel by Larry Watts

"It is only half-truths that are dangerous." *George Bernard Shaw*

First published by Larry Watts 2013

ISBN: 978-0-9890859-0-8

This is a work of fiction. All the characters depicted in this novel are fictional and are the product of the author's imagination. All events portrayed in the novel are also fictional, in part drawn from the author's more than 40 years working with the criminal justice system and in reading the published accounts of the growing number of persons convicted and later exonerated by Texas courts.

Printed in the United States of America

Published by Larry Dean Watts Publishing

Dedication

This novel is dedicated to the hard work of The Innocence Project in pursuing justice for those who have been failed by our justice system. It is also dedicated to those workers in the various branches of the criminal justice system who strive to place justice above high case clearance rates, conviction rates, and all the other impediments to assuring that all people are treated fairly by our system.

Special thanks to Bob Massey who assisted the author with great insight into the operations of the Texas prison system during the 1980's and early 1990's and to H.L. O'Neal who provided insight into the legal aspects of the criminal courts system in Texas

Finally, because the names and cases of Randall Dale Adams, Timothy Cole, Clarence Brantley, and Michael Morton represent to me the worst of our Texas system of justice, this writing is dedicated to the struggles they each endured.

THE CRIME

Chapter One

Bobby Jordan walked out the door to the garage, tapped the garage door opener on the wall and sat in his five year old Toyota pick-up truck. He backed out, pushed the button that was clipped to the driver's sun visor and as soon as he saw the door begin to close, drove away from his home.

He arrived at George's Independent Auto Supply store where he worked ten minutes later. Bobby was the assistant manager and usually worked the opening shift. He began his daily routine by turning on the neon sign in the large plate glass window, that when lit, announced the store was open for business.

After a short discussion regarding the previous day's business with the two counter salesmen who worked the morning shift with him, he walked into his office. Seated at his desk, Bobby resumed the task of closing the books on last month's sales, a task he had begun two days earlier on Monday.

Ten minutes later one of the salesmen called to him from the sales counter.

"Bobby, line two. Woman said it was a personal call."

Bobby smiled because he was sure it was his wife, Regina. She had recently stopped working as a bank teller to care for their first child, two year old Bobby Jr., who had been tagged from birth with the nickname of B.J. Regina sometimes called Bobby just to check in with him during the day. It was one of the benefits of having his wife staying home with their son. It seemed as if they were growing closer after several years of struggling to make their marriage successful. He picked up the receiver and punched the button for the line that was blinking.

"Good morning," he said in a cheerful voice.

"Mr. Jordan, this is Helen Johnson. I'm your neighbor, second house on the right. It's none of my business really, but are you aware that your son is playing in the front yard by himself? Like I said, it's none of my business but I rang your doorbell and there's no answer. I guess your wife is still asleep. I am worried about that child getting in the street."

Bobby's gut tightened.

"Mrs. Johnson, thank you for calling. I am on my way right now. Would you mind getting B.J. and taking him to your house? I can't imagine that Regina is still asleep but I'll be right there."

Helen Johnson assured him she would take the boy to her home. Bobby quickly replaced the phone and hurried out of the office. On his way out the back door to the employee parking lot, he told the two employees he had a little emergency at home and would be back in a few minutes.

As he drove he couldn't imagine what was going on. Regina would never allow their son to play in the front yard unless she was with him. As he turned onto their street, it appeared as the same quiet peaceful neighborhood he had left just less than an hour earlier. He parked in the drive and pressed the garage door opener. They never locked the door from the utility room to the garage. He was quickly inside the house.

"Regina?"

No answer as he walked from the utility room down the hall into the den. He noticed that the back door was open and quickly checked the small backyard. He saw B.J.'s favorite floppy-eared, stuffed blood hound lying on the grass by the open gate to the front yard. Obviously B.J. had managed to get into the front yard when he found the gate open.

Bobby re-entered the house through the den, calling for his wife as he walked toward the bedroom. The bedroom door was partially closed and when he pushed against it, he could feel something against the door creating a drag, but not heavy enough to prevent him from opening it. All his senses immediately became numb as he looked into the room.

There was blood splattered across the bed and onto two walls. He saw a woman's foot on the far side of the mattress and it appeared the rest of the body was on the floor hidden by the bed. As he walked around the bed, he fell to his knees in shock. Regina was lying on the floor with her body grossly contorted. One foot was on the bed, the other partially out of sight under the bed. Her left arm appeared to be disjointed from its normal connection to the rest of her body and twisted grotesquely behind her head. Regina's throat had been slashed and her eyes stared vacantly, but in horror, at the ceiling. Bobby rose and moved backward out of the bedroom.

As he moved into the alcove outside the bedroom door, he turned and ran from the house. He ran to the Johnson home and beat on the door before realizing there was a doorbell. He repeatedly pushed it until Helen Johnson opened the door. As soon as she saw him, she screamed and backed away. His face was contorted and there was blood on his right hand, shirt sleeve and both knees of his pants.

"Where's my son," he asked as he saw B.J. walking toward him from another room. He ran to his son, swept him into his arms and began crying.

Helen Johnson, however, had regained her composure.

"Mr. Jordan, what has happened?" she asked.

"Call the police and an ambulance. My wife is dead." Bobby told her through the barely controlled tears.

Helen Johnson ran to the phone and called 911. She quickly explained that something had happened at her neighbor's house, that she thought his wife might be dead and that she had their two year old son at her house. When she hung up the phone, she asked Bobby if she could get something for him to drink.

Bobby had regained some control of his emotions, at least outwardly; and he was no longer crying.

"No, thank you, Mrs. Johnson, but can you watch B.J. while I go to the house and meet with the police?"

The sound of sirens was increasing rapidly as a police car and ambulance turned off the main street into the sub-division.

"Mr. Jordan, don't worry about your son. Is there anyone you want me to call?" she asked.

"No. I will need to talk to Regina's mother myself. Thanks for helping. I'll be back here as soon as I finish with the police."

Chapter Two

As Bobby arrived back at the driveway of his home, two emergency vehicles rolled to a stop. A police officer and two paramedics exited the vehicles with the sense of urgency such emergency calls predict. The officer was the first to reach Bobby.

"What's happened here?" the officer asked.

"My wife is in the bedroom." Bobby said, pointing toward the house. "She's dead."

"What's your name?" The officer asked the question as the paramedics walked quickly toward the house with their small black medical bags in hand.

"I'm Bobby Jordan." He was becoming dizzy and could taste bitter bile at the back of his tongue. It felt as if he might vomit.

"Ok, Mr. Jordan. Come with me and let's see what we have," the officer commanded as he turned toward the house. He extended his hand in a gesture intended to let Bobby know that he would follow him into the house.

"I don't want to go back in there." Bobby shook his head and tears brimmed in his eyes as he told the officer. "I don't think I can handle it."

"Just come in the house. I won't ask you to go to the bedroom again." The officer took Bobby's arm and as he guided him toward the front door said, "By the way, I'm Officer Lance Walker. I don't think I introduced myself."

Once inside, the officer told Bobby to take a seat on the couch in the den and asked him which bedroom his wife was in. Before Bobby could respond, the paramedics walked from the bedroom with solemn facial expressions.

The older of the two motioned for the officer to follow him to the door and then spoke quietly so that Bobby did not hear what was said.

"It's a DOA. Pretty nasty scene in there. There's nothing we can do here. I'll call for a body car when we get back in service. Our unit number is 1254 if it's needed for the reports." With that the paramedics left the home.

Officer Walker strode into the bedroom and had a physical reaction to the scene even though he was accustomed to witnessing the aftermath of violence on a nearly daily basis. Just standing in the bedroom caused him to feel that something evil was still lurking unseen in the room.

He walked back to the den and asked Bobby where he might use the phone. Bobby pointed to a telephone on the kitchen bar. The officer dialed a number from memory. Patrol officers talked with the homicide office often during their tours of duty and the phone number stayed with many of them for years after they had retired.

When the clerk answered the phone he asked to speak to the lieutenant on duty.

"Lieutenant Kelner." The response was all business.

"Lieutenant, this is Walker, unit 2 Charley 13. I am on a call at 223 Pirtle Lane and I've got a homicide here. It's a nasty one; female, white, in her early thirties. The husband is here, but I haven't talked with him. Can you get a team out here along with the medical examiner's office?"

Walker spoke softly hoping that Bobby Jordan couldn't hear the conversation.

"I'll get 'em rolling." The lieutenant responded. "Keep the husband away from everyone until they arrive. You know the routine, Walker. Secure the scene and don't let anyone on the property."

When the detectives arrived, yellow crime scene tape encircled the front yard. They walked unannounced into the house where Bobby Jordan sat staring out the window into the back yard. Officer Walker was sitting at a small breakfast table filling out forms associated with the never-ending mass of bureaucratic paperwork associated with the job. Walker and the detectives stepped away from Jordan while the officer briefed the detectives about what he knew.

*****

Marcus Wilson had been a Houston police officer for twenty-nine years and a homicide detective for more than twenty. He was cynical, tired, and no longer enjoyed his work. Wilson's lack of interest was evident in his dismissive attitude and in eyes that were increasingly red-rimmed. His once finely chiseled facial features had become heavy and without tone. His blood pressure correlated with his weight, frustration with his work and after shift stops at a local *cop bar*.

He would have preferred to be shuffling paperwork on the hundreds of minor assault cases that came through the homicide division office while he counted the months until he would retire. But this morning, Lieutenant Pete Kelner had assigned him to work with detectives Starbuck and Lawson on the latest murder case.

T.J. Lawson was a brand new detective, having been promoted only three days earlier. Jimmy Starbuck had been working homicides for three years, but as Lieutenant Kelner had explained to Wilson, Starbuck, though thought to be an excellent investigator, was a self-promoting prick. The lieutenant didn't trust him to train the new detective without some oversight.

So the "Lew" had made the somewhat unusual decision to assign all three detectives to the case. What Lieutenant Kelner didn't tell Wilson was that he was also trying to push Wilson to make a choice to take some interest in his work, ask for a transfer from the homicide, or to retire. Making him work with the two younger detectives would at least require Wilson to leave the office.

"You the husband?" Wilson asked in a dry disinterested voice as he stood before Bobby Jordan.

Bobby looked up as if it was the first time he realized someone else had entered the room. He glanced at the other two detectives standing behind the man who had addressed him.

"I am," Bobby said with no emotion left in his voice. His body felt heavy; there was a ringing in his ears; and a dull pain at the nape of his neck. He forced himself to focus on the officer's words.

"What happened to your wife?" Wilson stood with his hands in his pockets, assuming that one of the younger detectives would make any notes they deemed necessary.

"I don't know," Bobby stuttered and then he hesitantly revealed the events of the morning to the detective.

As he finished talking, the crime scene units arrived and Detectives Starbuck and Lawson assisted them in setting up to work the scene. Detective Wilson, however, sat in a recliner across from the couch where Bobby was seated and said nothing more until his two new partners returned.

"Ok," said Detective Starbuck, "They are working the room and we've found what appears to be the murder weapon. It's a Rapala brand filleting knife. I just bought one myself at Academy last week. Mr. Jordan, is it your knife?"

"I don't know. I have a filleting knife that I keep with the other knives in the kitchen, but it was a gift and I couldn't tell you what brand it is or where it was bought."

Detective Starbuck stared thoughtfully for a moment at Bobby Jordan. If Starbuck had known what the Lieutenant said about him earlier that morning, he would have disagreed. He considered himself a very good investigator and believed he could read people better than anyone he had ever worked with. If you are that good, he believed, you don't have to be a self-promoter.

"Alright then, I want Detective Lawson to take you to our office and get a detailed statement from you about what happened here. Wilson, you mind going down and talking to this neighbor, Mrs. Johnson, and getting a statement from her?"

Wilson looked at Starbuck with contempt. Obviously Jimmy Starbuck was taking the lead on this case. That was alright with Marcus Wilson, but he wasn't so sure about taking orders from the younger detective, especially if the orders involved more work. He was also not happy that since Lawson was taking the husband to the station, Starbuck would need to ride back with him. He preferred the freedom of working alone, which is why he had declined the offer to ride with the other two detectives to the scene of the crime.

But before Wilson could voice an objection, Bobby Jordan spoke.

"I'm sorry detective, but I've got to contact my wife's family, let my boss know what's going on and get my son from Mrs. Johnson. I can't go to your office until I take care of that."

"Mr. Jordan, your wife has been murdered. We're trying to figure out who did it and we need your undivided attention. So call whoever you want, make your arrangements and then we'll go downtown. But let's get moving."

Jimmy Starbuck believed it was important to be in charge. He also loved getting credit for solving murder cases and for anything else that got him interviews with the media. What he didn't like was to be told no.

"I'm sorry. I didn't mean I wouldn't help. I am just a little confused right now."

Bobby stood and went to the same phone the officer had used earlier. He dialed his wife's parents' number and began speaking. As he spoke he became more distraught, but in a short time hung the phone back on the wall.

"My mother-in-law is on the way here. She'll take B.J. with her. I'll call my neighbor, Mrs. Johnson, and let her know that Regina's mom will pick B.J. up.

After I do that and call my boss I can go with the detective."

That said, Bobby called Mrs. Johnson with the information that Regina's mother would be coming to get B.J. He then dialed a second number and after a short conversation that ended with him telling the person on the line there was nothing he could do to help right now, he hung up the phone and returned to the couch.

In the next few moments, Wilson left for the Johnson home, having decided not to argue with Starbuck at this juncture. T.J. Lawson introduced himself to Bobby Jordan and suggested they leave for the station. Bobby complied with the request, happy to be leaving the home where so much had happened in the last few hours.

Chapter Three

When they arrived at the station, Detective Lawson took Bobby Jordan to a small interrogation room. Not unsympathetic to Bobby's current emotional condition, he worked with him slowly to get all the details about the morning's events into a statement which Bobby read and signed. The detective then took Bobby back to his home which now was quiet; all the investigators having finished working the crime scene. Bobby immediately went to his truck and drove away without entering the house.

He couldn't get his thoughts together. Until now, all his activities seemed to have been directed by the detectives. On his own again, he could think of only one place to go. Jack and Linda Seneca were Bobby's closest relatives in Houston. Linda, his sister, was two years older than Bobby. She and Jack lived only a few miles from his home. His brother Dale lived in the Houston area also, but his home was further away in the suburban town of Sugarland, southwest of Houston.

When he arrived at the Seneca home all the emotions of the morning were relived as he told Linda of the morning's events. Although she was shocked by the revelations, she handled her emotions by taking charge.

First, she called Regina's mother and told her that she would bring Bobby to pick up B.J. in a couple of hours. Regina's mother, Jenny White, wanted information. She was in shock and wanted details. Linda assured her that Bobby would talk to her when they arrived.

Linda then called Dale at work; he agreed to leave work early and meet them at Linda's home. After Dale arrived and Bobby repeated the day's events again, the three of them settled into a less emotional conversation.

Linda was the glue that kept the three siblings in contact with each other. She was the oldest and felt some responsibility for her two brothers. Before she had a chance to speak, however, Dale blurted out a question.

"Bobby, why would anyone have done this?" Dale asked. "Was it a burglar?"

"Dale, leave him alone! He doesn't know why anyone would do something like this." Linda was clearly irritated at the question.

"I just thought that maybe there's been an argument or some conflict that might explain why someone would want to hurt her. I am sure the police are going to ask the same question," Dale responded.

"I told the police I can't think of anything to help them. No arguments with neighbors. You know Regina wasn't a person who enjoyed conflict. I just don't know," Bobby said.

"What about you two? I know you guys had patched things up, but were you getting along ok?"

The question from Dale drew an immediate response from Linda. "I can't believe you just asked that. Leave him alone, Dale. You're not helping at all."

"Look, I'm just trying to understand this. We all know that Bobby and Regina have had their share of problems. I know things have been better for the last couple of years since B.J. was born, but I'm just asking," Dale retorted.

"Our deal has been better than ever before," Bobby said. "I know we argued and were separated for a while, but that was all behind us. Look, I need to get out of here...go and get B.J."

Bobby stood, but before he could move away from the chair Linda was beside him. "I'll drive you," she said emphatically.

Bobby and Dale hugged and shook hands. "I didn't mean to say anything to hurt you," Dale said as Bobby turned to leave.

*****

Upon arrival at the White residence, Jenny White met them in the yard as they exited the car. She was a small, plump woman who had attended the Baptist church faithfully since her earliest memory. She was quick to smile, but those who knew her best, realized that she had a very strict set of values except where her daughter was concerned. She had been adept at rationalizing her daughter's behavior as acceptable since Regina was a very small child.

"Bobby, what happened? My little girl can't be dead! I just talked to her last night. Tell me." There was a combination of grief and anger in Jenny White's voice.

Bobby again went over the details as he knew them, after which his sister, Linda, suggested they discuss funeral arrangements. While they were engaged in this conversation, Jenny White received a call from Detective Starbuck, who began asking questions about Bobby and Regina's relationship. Starbuck quickly realized that Bobby was probably in the room with Mrs. White. He asked to meet with her at noon the following day.

Chapter Four

On Thursday, the day after the murder, the three detectives and Lieutenant Kelner met in the Lieutenant's office to review the investigation. Such meetings were routine with potentially high profile murder cases that might attract a lot of media attention.

The police chief and mayor did not like news coverage of crime in Houston that raised the level of voters' anxiety, especially if they included unsolved murders. Lieutenant Kelnar knew he would be held accountable for any such coverage which occurred if the case wasn't solved promptly. At this point, the media had simply made initial reports of a woman murdered in her home and the police investigating. Kellner knew, however, that reporters would be in his office before the day was over wanting details, including who the suspect was.

"So what have we got on this one?" the Lieutenant began. "Sign of forced entry? Domestic problems? Any property stolen from the home?"

Jimmy Starbuck thought he knew what the boss was looking for. "I think our suspect is the husband. He didn't seem all that concerned about helping us when we got to the house. No forced entry and we don't know of any missing property." Starbuck sat back in his chair and folded his arms across his chest as if daring someone to challenge his assertion.

Rookie Detective T.J. Lawson looked at the senior investigator, Marcus Wilson. Wilson was cleaning his fingernails with a small pocket knife and appeared to be oblivious to the discussion.

"So, what does the husband look like? Does he have a record?" Lieutenant Kellner continued his questioning.

This time the rookie spoke up. "I checked his record. He was arrested for "joy-riding" when he was seventeen. I pulled up the report. He was with three friends who stole a Camaro, drove it around half the night and then ran it into a retention pond south of town. He got deferred adjudication and has nothing else in the system except for two speeding tickets and a minor accident that he was ticketed for."

"Ok, what'd the neighbor say who found the little boy?" Kellner looked at Wilson.

"She saw the kid, called the husband who asked her to go get the kid and watch him until the husband could get there. Said she didn't see anybody else around the house, but she heard the husband's truck when he left for work earlier in the morning, about 6:45, she said."

Wilson folded his pocket knife and looked out the window over the Lieutenant's left shoulder.

"Anything else from her?" Kellner persisted.

"Not really." Wilson turned his gaze to the Lieutenant. "She said when Jordan beat on the door she opened it and was scared because he looked like a crazy man with blood all over him. She really doesn't know the family all that well. Sees him working in the yard occasionally and has gossiped with the wife a few times."

"So he was covered with blood?" The Lieutenant leaned forward in his chair.

"That's what she said." Wilson responded.

T.J. Lawson could not contain himself any longer. To hell with the fact he was the rookie.

"Bobby Jordan was not covered in blood. We all saw him just after the neighbor did. He had blood on the knees of his pants and on his right shirt sleeve. None of it was splattered. It was more like it was smeared; consistent with his having knelt beside his wife's body and moving a wisp of hair that had fallen across her mouth. That's how he explained it to me during the interrogation."

T.J. felt better. He wasn't happy with himself for having remained silent when Starbuck declared Jordan to be the suspect.

The Lieutenant appeared to ignore T.J.'s assertions and looked back at Wilson. "Ok, what about the family? How was the marriage going? Was money a problem for them? Any insurance on the victim?"

Starbuck chose to answer. "I talked briefly to the mother by phone but Jordan was there with her, so I am meeting her at noon today."

"Ok, T.J. you need to do a financial work-up on Bobby Jordan. Find out who he owes money to, if he gambles or has any other expensive hobbies, including girlfriends. Wilson, you interview his boss and all his co-workers. Find out everything they know. If this guy is our suspect, I want to know everything there is to know about him.

"We meet at four this afternoon. I know you won't have everything tied up, but the media will be driving me crazy. I need enough to at least tell them that the husband is a *person of interest* in the investigation." The Lieutenant stood behind his desk as if to indicate the meeting was over.

"Don't you think we ought to canvass the streets in the neighborhood to see if anyone saw anything suspicious?" T.J. asked.

Wilson, who had already started walking out of the room, stopped and turned.

"You know what, rookie. This ain't a cop show on television. We got a suspect; let's not create work for ourselves. If he's not the one, we'll figure it out."

As T.J. walked out of the office, red-faced from the put-down by Wilson, he wished he had drawn a different case on his third day as a detective. It was obvious that Wilson just wanted to avoid doing any extra work on the case. Starbuck, for whatever reason, had already decided who the murderer was and the Lieutenant was more than happy with this as long as he had an answer for the media. It was disturbing, but he also realized that he was the rookie. These guys must know what they are doing.

Chapter Five

As the second-hand on the clock in the lieutenant's office ticked toward four o'clock, the detectives drifted back in one at a time. They each took notes from their pockets as they sat in the chairs positioned in front of Kellner's desk.

"So what do we have, guys? Jimmy, did you talk to the mother?" the Lieutenant asked.

Starbuck didn't look at his notes. "I did and it's pretty interesting. She told me that Jordan and her daughter have had some problems in the past. They've been married for nearly six years. She says they separated several times before the kid was born a couple of years ago. I asked her if Jordan was ever violent with her daughter and she said she didn't know. She said her daughter probably wouldn't have told her if he had been.

"She did tell me the daughter didn't want to quit work but that Jordan insisted she stay home with their son. She had talked to the mother about going back to work recently, but the mother didn't know if her daughter had talked to Jordan."

"Is that it?" the Lieutenant asked.

"Well, she wanted to know if we thought he was the one who killed her daughter. I thought that was pretty revealing about what she thinks."

Jimmy Starbuck glanced at the other two detectives as he said this.

"Alright then," the Lieutenant shifted his gaze to Detective Lawson. "Lawson, what did you come up with on their financial situation?"

T.J. Lawson flipped the small notebook open that he had used to take notes earlier in the day. "Well, of course we will have to subpoena any actual financial records we want to look at, but I spoke to a couple of neighbors. They say Bobby Jordan is a hard worker and doesn't seem to spend a lot of money, but he does play in a neighborhood poker game once a month. One guy, a neighbor who plays the same game, said no one ever loses more than about a hundred bucks or so.

This neighbor, Jackie Anderson, says he thinks Bobby's truck is paid for, but that last year he bought his wife a new Corvette convertible and probably owes money on it. They bought the house but are like everyone else, just making payments hoping to really own it someday.

I did pick up one more piece of info when I was interviewing the neighbors. A woman, Mrs. Greene, who lives on the street behind the Jordan's home, saw a little burgundy colored foreign car parked just down the street, which would have been pretty much directly behind the Jordan home, when she went outside at about 6:30 yesterday morning. She didn't recognize the car, said it didn't belong in the neighborhood, and it was gone when she went back out at about 8:30."

"So did you talk to the district attorney about getting a subpoena for the bank records?" the Lieutenant asked.

"I haven't yet. I spend most of the day out in the neighborhood. I can do that first thing tomorrow."

T.J. was disappointed that there appeared to be no interest at all about the unfamiliar car in the neighborhood.

"Ok, Wilson. What have you got?"

Kellner was ready to get this meeting over. He had told two television reporters he would give them an interview for their Live at Five news casts and he needed a few minutes to prepare.

"Well, I talked to Jordan's boss who thinks Jordan hung the moon. Says Bobby Jordan loved his wife, but loved his son more than anything. He didn't know of any problems. Same story from all the guys who work with him. They didn't have anything bad to say. One of the guys mentioned that Jordan had legal troubles years ago, but that's all." Wilson was ready for the meeting to end also.

"I have an update on the physical evidence from the crime scene techs." the Lieutenant began.

"The murder weapon was recovered as you know. It was the fillet knife found at the scene. They also tagged a pull-over Oilers football sweater that was partially under the bedroom door. It had her blood on it and probably belongs to the husband. They lifted several prints in the bedroom and so far all of the prints belong to either Bobby or Regina Jordan. I think the physical evidence is shaping up to fit Starbuck's theory that the husband did it."

"Are they doing any DNA testing on the knife or anything else at the scene?" T.J. Lawson asked.

The Lieutenant smiled as he looked at Lawson. The use of DNA evidence in criminal cases was a recent addition to the tools that science had provided law enforcement. The first conviction using DNA evidence had occurred in 1987, just three years before. Most officers and a few detectives still didn't understand much about the use of DNA evidence.

"You've been doing your homework I guess, T.J. The answer is probably not, since we seem to be putting together a pretty good case on a guy whose DNA is all over that room. It's expensive. It takes time to get it done, and in this case probably wouldn't add anything to our case.

Alright, I'm doing an interview for a couple of television stations at five. Why don't you guys hang around and be there with me just in case there's something I need from you." The lieutenant again ended the meeting by standing behind his desk.

The three detectives filed out of his office and as soon as they were in the hallway, Wilson said, "I can't believe this! We stay here to hold his hand and I'll be in afternoon traffic for an hour trying to get home. I thought 4 o'clock was too late for this meeting, but staying for the media is ridiculous."

Jimmy Starbuck grinned at Wilson.

"Marcus, how long has it been since you stayed here for a full shift? I bet by now you're usually home drinking a cold beer and practicing your golf swing in the back yard."

The three detectives went separate ways, knowing they would be back together in less than thirty minutes serving as a backdrop to the Lieutenants press conference.

*****

At five o'clock all three detectives stood behind the Lieutenant in the media conference room as he began the media update. A Chronicle reporter, two news radio reporters and four local television news crews were there for the update.

"Ladies and gentlemen, I know you want an update on our latest homicide. As you know, I always try to give you as much information as I can release just as soon as I can without jeopardizing our investigation. In this case it is very early in the investigation but I can tell you this.

"Detective Jimmy Starbuck and I will meet with the district attorney tomorrow and discuss filing charges in this case. If he agrees with our assessment, we will file charges and make an arrest before this time tomorrow. I am sure you will understand that I can't tell you more until we meet with the district attorney. Thank you."

"Are you arresting the husband?" a well-coiffed female television reporter stepped close to the podium as she asked the question.

The lieutenant and detectives turned without answering and exited the room from a side door that led back to their offices.

Detective T.J. Lawson was shocked. He thought the investigation had just begun and the lieutenant had already announced a possible arrest. But more surprises were in store for the rookie detective.

Chapter Six

As the door closed behind them, the Lieutenant turned to address the trio. "Ok, Lawson, you go with Starbuck. We're bringing Bobby Jordan in to answer some questions. Wilson, you can go home. I heard what you said about having to stay for the news conference. If you're not interested in working homicides, you need to look for an assignment somewhere else. This isn't a semi-retirement job."

Wilson was surprised by the Lieutenant's attitude. They had known each other for years. "Lew, I'm ok with the five o'clock news conference. I was just blowing off steam."

With that Wilson silently accepted the offer to go home, although he wouldn't be so quick to follow up on the suggestion that he find another assignment.

*****

After Jimmy Starbuck and T.J. Lawson were in the car and driving toward Bobby Jordan's home, T.J. began with a question. "Jimmy, what are we doing? We haven't wrapped up this investigation and we are already arresting a suspect."

Starbuck kept his eyes on the road as he answered. "Look, T.J., we need to wrap this up and get this guy off the streets. We'll bring him in, get another statement from him and, with any luck, he'll give it up. I know he killed his wife. I've got an instinct for these things. Just come along and watch how it's done. This will be good training."

They parked in the drive of the Jordan home. When Bobby answered the door, Jimmy Starbuck advised him that he needed to come with them to the station to discuss his wife's murder in more detail. Bobby Jordan complied with their request after making arrangements for his mother-in-law to watch his son. Less than an hour after the news conference had ended, Starbuck and Lawson were sitting across from him in one of several interrogation rooms within the homicide division office.

Starbuck began the conversation. "Ok, Jordan. Let's cut to the chase. Here's the way I see it. You say you left for work on the morning of your wife's murder and everything was alright. A witness says you left at 6:45 that morning. At about 8:40 your neighbor calls 911 and reports the murder and you say you found the body after she called and told you the boy was in your front yard. That sound about right to you?"

Bobby Jordan could sense that Detective Starbuck was not his friend in the matter of his wife's death. "That's what happened," he replied.

"Well, here's what's wrong with your story. First, you and your wife have had some pretty serious problems. You separated several times before your son was born and then you insisted that your wife quit work although she didn't want to. She's been talking about going back to work, but you wouldn't hear of it. More arguments and she even told her mother she wants to go back to work."

Bobby Jordan interrupted Starbuck. "Wait a minute. Where are you getting all this? My wife wasn't going back to work. We weren't having serious problems. In fact, things were going better than they ever had since B.J. was born."

"Stick with that story and you'll be on death row before you know it," Starbuck responded. "You got up that morning and made sure your son was still asleep, woke your wife and argued with her about going back to work. It got physical and you lost it. She fought you and you used the knife to cut her throat. Beat her pretty bad before that though. The only thing I'm curious about is why you left your son there. A jury sure isn't going to like the idea of a two year old being left to find his mother's body. So you want to tell us about it?"

Bobby Jordan sat back in his chair. He couldn't remember ever having thought that he hated somebody, but that had just changed. He couldn't believe anyone could be so cruel.

"I told Detective Lawson what happened in my statement. I am not going to sit here and listen to you talking such trash." He began to rise from the chair.

"Sit down! We're not through with you." Starbuck's facial expression caused Bobby Jordan to slump back into his chair.

"My partner is going to take you over to the courthouse and get a judge to read you your rights. Now once that's done you have two choices. First, you can lawyer up and he'll tell you not to talk to us. If you do that, we'll just file charges and you can talk to a judge and jury about what really happened. The second choice is for you to help us with this and if it happened the way you say, you get to go home."

Bobby Jordan was having trouble grasping what was happening to him. He wanted to help solve the murder of his wife, but he was convinced there was nothing he could say to Jimmy Starbuck that would convince the detective he was not his wife's killer.

Detective Lawson stood and motioned for Bobby Jordan to come with him. They took the elevator to the main lobby and then walked out the front doors of the police station and across the street to the municipal courts building.

Once in the courthouse, Lawson peered in the small window on the doors of two courtrooms before finding one where a judge was on the bench conducting business. He walked in with Jordan, directed him to sit on the front bench and asked the court clerk for a Miranda warning form. Once he had filled in the blanks on the form he returned it to the court clerk and took a seat beside Jordan while they waited for a break in the speeding ticket case the judge was dealing with.

In a few minutes the judge declared that he found the errant driver guilty, assessed a fine and picked up the form the clerk handed him.

"Detective Lawson, bring your suspect to the bench please," the judge directed.

The detective and Bobby Jordan stood before the judge as he read the now universally well-known Miranda rights to Jordan, advising him that he didn't have to talk to detectives, he had a right to talk to a lawyer and so on. Upon completing his reading, he looked at Jordan and asked if he understood his rights and if he had any questions. When Bobby responded that he did understand his rights and had no questions, Lawson took his arm and directed him out of the courtroom.

As they walked back toward the police station, Bobby Jordan began talking to Lawson. "The other detective seemed to be telling me that I should keep talking to you guys. Do you think that's what I should do?" he asked.

"That's up to you, Mr. Jordan. You heard what the judge said." T.J. Lawson did not like the question.

"Oh, I understood what the judge said, but I need advice. I can't believe you guys think I killed my wife. I want to do the right thing."

Jordan wanted help and T.J. Lawson knew his partner would expect him to encourage the suspect to continue talking to them. "You know what? That's up to you. You won't hurt my feelings if you decide to talk to a lawyer first, but that's up to you. If you want advice, get a lawyer."

That was the best Lawson could do without feeling that he had betrayed his partner. Nothing else was said until they were back in the interrogation room.

Starbuck resumed questioning Bobby as if the interruption had never taken place. "Jordan, we need to go over your story again. I'm just having trouble believing you," he began.

But Bobby Jordan had made his decision. "I'm sorry, detective, but I've said all I am going to say to you until after I have hired a lawyer and talked to him."

"Well, if that's the way you want to play it, go ahead, but you're making a big mistake. You'll get no more help from me."

Starbuck would walk the line of legality. If Bobby Jordan continued to talk without being questioned, Starbuck would ignore his statement about wanting a lawyer. But that wasn't to be.

Bobby looked at each of them and said, "So unless I am under arrest, I'd like to go home. If I am under arrest, I want an opportunity to use the phone."

"I'll take you home," Lawson said before Jimmy Starbuck could attempt to begin another conversation.

T.J. Lawson drove in silence. He would have liked to tell Jordan he thought he made the right decision, but there was something about saying it that would have seemed disloyal to his partners and his lieutenant.

Chapter Seven

Bobby Jordan had begun sleeping in the guest bedroom of his home after the murder. On Friday morning he was out of bed and drinking coffee by five-thirty. He felt better than he had since discovering Regina's body. He had things to do. First, he would go to the funeral home and finalize arrangements for tomorrow's memorial service, after which he would call the lawyer whose name his boss had given him.

George had hired the guy to represent his son once on a driving while intoxicated charge and said he did a good job for his son. Bobby recognized the man's name, Jefferson Clay, because he had represented a number of wealthy clients in Houston whose crimes garnered considerable press coverage. As a result, Clay was often interviewed by local news reporters.

Just after seven, Bobby helped B.J. get dressed and explained to him that he would be staying with Aunt Linda for the day. B.J. had been asking where his mother was and Bobby intended to have a talk with him upon returning from the day's activities. In the meantime, B.J. loved visiting with his Aunt Linda and was excited about the adventure.

After dropping his son at his sister's home, Bobby met his mother-in-law at the funeral home. They had previously agreed there would be a memorial service on Saturday afternoon and the body would be cremated. The director of the funeral home advised that he expected the medical examiner to release the body sometime before five that afternoon. He told them that as soon as his staff could transport the body from the county morgue, the cremation procedure would begin and the remains would be available in an urn for the service on Saturday. As Bobby and Jenny walked to their cars, he asked her how she was doing.

"I'm coping," she said curtly. "You know that detective told me he thinks you killed Regina, don't you?"

"I know one of the detectives thinks that. Surely you don't believe I could ever have hurt her, do you?" Bobby stopped walking and stared at her.

"I don't know what to believe, Bobby. I'm numb. I want my daughter back. But there must be some reason they think you did it."

With that Jenny turned, walked the few feet to her car, quickly opened the door, sat in the driver's seat and in moments was driving away.

*****

Bobby called the lawyer, Jefferson Clay, when he returned home. After hearing Bobby's story, Clay suggested Bobby come to his office as soon as he could. By eleven o'clock, the two of them sat across from each other in a conference room in the offices of Woodrow, Clay and De Jarnett.

After Bobby related all the events he could remember, Clay began. "I know you want to explain all this again to the detectives, Bobby, but I am going to advise you not to. Whether you talk to them or not, they are likely to charge you with your wife's murder.

No need to help them try to make a case. What you need to do today is make arrangements for someone to watch your son just in case they come to your house to arrest you. I'll call Pete Kellner. He's the lieutenant who held the press conference yesterday. I'll advise him you have retained my services and I don't want his guys talking to you." Clay smiled. "Just remember, sometimes they don't do what I tell them, so if they call you or show up at your house, don't talk. If they arrest you, call me and I will get bail set for you."

"I'll do what you say, Mr. Clay. Is there anything else I need to do?" Bobby was relieved to have someone finally who was on his side.

"Well, there is one thing," Jefferson Clay responded. "This could very well be a capital murder case and they are expensive. I'll need a five thousand dollar retainer to get us through indictment. If you aren't indicted, that will cover everything. If they do indict you, you'll need another fifty thousand for my fee and probably fifteen to twenty for an investigator, expert testimony and such. So be thinking about that."

"Wow, I haven't even thought about money. I have nearly five thousand in savings. I don't know about the rest, but I'll try to figure it out."

It was more money than Bobby had ever spent on anything except his house and Regina's Corvette, but even then he only had to have about three thousand dollars in cash for the house and no cash down on the car since he had a trade-in.

"Take it one step at a time. Let's see what happens." Jefferson Clay stood and walked around the table. They shook hands and Bobby left the office.

*****

The homicide investigation was progressing swiftly. Lieutenant Kellner had the three detectives in his office at eight the next morning. They discussed the previous evening's interrogation of Jordan after which the lieutenant focused the conversation on the evidence.

"Here's what we have. The medical examiner's report doesn't indicate a sexual assault, although her panties were around her left ankle. She was beaten about the head and shoulders severely and it appears there was a ferocious battle between the deceased and the murderer during which her left arm was pulled from the socket. The murder weapon was confirmed to be the filleting knife found by the door. As you all know there was no forced entry into the home and Jordan told us the house was locked when he left. Crime scene folks took scrapings from under the victim's fingernails, but there was no evidence of her having scratched the suspect."

T.J. Lawson asked the first question. "Why would her husband pull her panties down? That doesn't make sense to me."

"There is always the possibility the confrontation occurred as she was putting them on and just never got them pulled up." Jimmy Starbuck responded. "T.J., what's up with you trying to defend this guy? It looks pretty cut and dried to me."

The lieutenant spoke again. "Well, if it's not cut and dried, it's getting close. The victim's mother called yesterday. She said Bobby Jordan had been suspicious that his wife was fooling around with the salesman they bought her Corvette from. She said her daughter had asked her to ride with her when she took the car in for an oil change because she didn't want Jordan accusing her of going there to see the salesman.

"So, Jimmy, let's go see Bradley V. and try to convince him there's enough to charge this guy. While we're meeting with the district attorney, it wouldn't hurt for you two to pay a visit to the car salesman. See what he knows and what he'll say about his relationship with Regina Jordan."

The lieutenant's secretary tapped on the door as she stepped into the room. "Jefferson Clay is on line one. He says he needs to talk with you, lieutenant."

Kellner reached for the phone. "Pete Kellner here."

"Pete, Jefferson Clay. I just wanted to let you know that Bobby Jordan is now my client. Thought you might tell me where you guys are going with this thing."

Kellner smiled as he answered. "Well, Jefferson, I didn't know Jordan had the kinda' dough it takes to get a lawyer with your credentials, but to answer your question, we're going to solve the murder of Mrs. Jordan. You and your client plan on helping us with that?"

Jefferson Clay ignored the comment about his client's financial affairs. "You know we will cooperate with the investigation in every way, except that my client will not have any further discussions with you or your boys unless I am with him. I would ask that you let them know they need to stay away from him."

"So he won't help us solve the murder of his wife?" Kellner enjoyed the banter with defense lawyers and was considered by most of them to be professional in his dealings, even though his remarks could at times be irritating.

"You lost that chance when you took Bobby to a judge and read him his rights. Anyway, just wanted to let you know he's my client. If you decide to charge him, let me know and I'll see that he makes bond. No need to make a big deal about arresting him publicly is there?"

Clay knew he wouldn't get much from Kellner but even a phone call at the same time or shortly after an arrest was made would give him an opportunity to get Bobby Jordan out of jail more quickly than if he waited on a call from the jail.

Chapter Eight

Friday afternoon was busy for Lieutenant Kellner and his detectives. He and Starbuck drove seven blocks to the criminal courts building where they discussed the case with District Attorney Bradley Vance Thompson.

"Look guys, I don't think you're ready yet with this case. You really don't have much at all. If you could have just gotten an admission from the husband it would be fine." Thompson was not happy with the case that had been presented to him.

"Well, Bradley V., it's all we are probably going to get. Bobby Jordan has lawyered up and hired Jefferson Clay. That's enough to tell you he did it. A guy like Jordan can't afford Clay unless he knows he's got real problems," Kellner responded.

Pete Kellner and Bradley Vance Thompson were old acquaintances. They had begun their careers in government within months of each other. Thompson began as a young municipal court prosecutor where he handled traffic tickets and public intoxication cases; Kellner as a rookie police officer wrote many of the tickets and arrested the drunks that provided a case load for the prosecutor. Virtually no one else took the liberty of addressing Thompson as Bradley V., and Thompson wished that Pete Kellner would show the same respect.

At the end of the meeting, Thompson prevailed. The lieutenant would announce that the husband of the deceased was a person of interest and they would see what the car salesman had to say. Kellner knew that almost anything more to bolster the case would be enough to file the charge. The district attorney wouldn't want to reject the case twice.

*****

When the lieutenant and Starbuck had left the homicide office to go to see the district attorney, T.J. Lawson suggested to Marcus Wilson that they drive out to the car dealership where Jordan had bought the Corvette and talk to the salesman.

"Lawson, surely you can handle an interview with a car salesman without me holding your hand." Wilson intended to start his weekend early this afternoon and hanging out with the younger detective wasn't part of his plans.

"No problem. I was just doing what the Lieutenant suggested," Lawson responded. With that he gathered his file and headed out the door.

*****

Marcus Wilson leaned back in the swivel chair he sat in and put his feet on the desk top. He picked up the morning newspaper and began looking through the advertisements. Wilson intended to spend the weekend relaxing in his backyard and needed to find a good price on Bud Light. His shopping was interrupted a few minutes later when the lieutenant's secretary transferred a phone call to his desk.

"Detective Wilson," he answered in a bored monotone.

"Detective, this is Jenny White. I am the mother of Regina Jordan who was murdered. I asked for Detective Starbuck who talked to me yesterday, but they said he wasn't in and that you were working on the case with him." The mother would have been surprised to see the disgusted frown that appeared on Marcus Wilson's face.

"What can I do for you?" Wilson asked dryly.

"Well, I know Detective Starbuck thinks my son-in-law murdered my daughter, but I need him to know that when I was keeping my grandson, B.J., he told me something I think may be important. I asked him what happened to his mother and he said a monster hurt her. I asked him if the monster was his daddy and he said 'no, daddy went to work' so I thought you guys would want to know that, since B.J. was home with his mother that morning," Jenny White paused.

"O.k., I got it. I'll pass it on to Starbuck, but don't worry too much about it. How old is the kid? Just about two isn't he? He probably was just scared because of whatever he saw." Wilson made a short note, hung up the phone and placed the note on Starbuck's desk. Thirty minutes later, Marcus Wilson was in his car headed home.

*****

T.J. Lawson pulled into the parking lot of the car dealership; before he was out of the car, a salesman was at his side. "I'm not a customer." Lawson cut off any opportunity for a sales pitch. "I need to speak to the salesman who sold a Corvette to a Bobby Jordan last year." As he spoke, Lawson held his police identification out for the man to see.

"That's the guy whose wife was killed. We were just talking about that this morning. Jerry Smith sold him that 'vetted'. Come on, I'll introduce you."

The salesman turned and walked toward the showroom as Lawson followed. "Hey Jerry, this cop needs to talk to you."

A tall, well-groomed man, who appeared to be approximately thirty years old, turned and faced the detective. "Yes sir. How can I help you?" He held out his hand and the detective shook it.

"Did you sell a Corvette to Bobby Jordan last year?" Lawson asked.

"I did and I heard about his wife being murdered. I figured you guys would be coming around to talk to me."

"Why would you think we would want to talk to you?" Lawson asked.

"Well, I know that Bobby and his wife were having some problems and Bobby thought I was trying to put a move on her. I figured it was just a matter of time before he told you something about me." Jerry Smith was unabashed in making the statement.

"And what was your relationship with Mrs. Jordan?" T.J. Lawson's interest had suddenly heightened.

"Oh, she was a little flirty when they came in to buy the car and she called me a couple of times afterward, but it was always under the pretense of asking a question about the Corvette.

"We talked a little and she told me her husband was jealous. Apparently she got caught several years ago in a similar situation with some guy," Jerry Smith continued.

"Did you two ever meet other than here at the dealership?" Lawson was watching Jerry Smith closely now.

"Nope, never did. You know, this job gives me plenty of opportunities to score with women. Bored housewives whose husbands aren't the jealous type, college girls and single women who just want an overnighter pass through here looking at cars every week. I don't need the misery of dealing with a jealous husband," Smith replied.

"You know anything about the guy you say Mrs. Jordan had the affair with several years ago?" Lawson asked.

"No. She came in for an oil change one day and I talked with her for a few minutes. She had her mother with her in the waiting area. She saw me out on the showroom floor and came out to say hi. She told me her mother was her alibi. I didn't understand and she explained that her husband was jealous because several years ago he had learned that she stopped after work for a drink with a male friend from work. She said he just wouldn't let it go, so to keep from being accused of coming in to flirt with me, she had her mother ride with her. That's all I know." Smith's confident manner never wavered as he continued answering questions.

"Ok," Lawson said. "I don't have anything else right now." He held out his hand and the two shook hands again. The detective turned to leave, then paused, turned back to Smith and asked, "Jerry, you ever had any trouble with the law?"

"Not really. Oh, I had an arrest for driving under the influence when I was 21, but nothing else."

"Ok, thanks for the time." Lawson turned and walked to his car.

*****

On Saturday, the memorial service for Regina Jordan was held. The chapel was packed with family and friends. Bobby spoke to both parents and received a polite, but cool, response. After the funeral he returned home with B.J.

Once at home, Bobby tried to explain what had happened to B.J., but was reasonably sure that, at best, the two-year old probably only understood that his Mommy was not coming back. He hoped that it might be a blessing his son was too young to understand.

Chapter Nine

When T.J. Lawson arrived in the homicide office on Monday morning, the lieutenant's secretary told him that Lieutenant Kellner wanted a meeting with the Jordan murder team in his office at eight fifteen. That gave him fifteen minutes to get a cup of coffee and look over his notes.

After pouring his coffee in the break room, he walked to his desk which was situated in a cubicle that contained four work stations. Marcus Wilson was at his desk in the cubicle with his feet in the chair in front of Jimmy Starbuck's desk. He was reading the sports section of the Houston Chronicle.

"Lieutenant wants to see us in a few minutes," T.J. Lawson said. "I hope Jimmy isn't running late."

"Oh, he's not late. He's in the Lew's office already. I'm sure he's helping Pete decide what he wants us to do on the Jordan case today. He's beginning to make me think he wants to run everybody's business." Marcus Wilson's tone was even more disgruntled than usual this morning.

T.J. was learning to ignore such comments from Wilson. Seconds later, Jimmy Starbuck opened the door and stepped just outside the Lieutenant's office.

"Hey you guys. Come on. The Lieutenant wants to get this meeting started."

After they were all seated in front of his desk, Lieutenant Kellner looked at Wilson and asked, "So what did we learn from the car salesman?"

Even as a rookie detective, T.J. knew part of his job was to cover his partners. "I have it right here, Marcus." He flipped a page on his note pad and began.

"Jerry Smith. That's the salesman's name. He's a typical car salesman. Well dressed, flashy smile and too much confidence. He said he's been expecting us to come by ever since he heard about the murder.

He confirmed what Jenny White told Jimmy. Bobby Jordan was jealous of him because he thought Regina and Jerry had something going on. Jerry says that she was flirting with him, but he didn't bite. Says he doesn't have time to deal with jealous husbands and gets plenty of opportunity with less risk from other female customers."

"Is that it?" the lieutenant asked.

"Just about all he said. He did tell me that Regina brought her mother with her once when she came in to get an oil change. That's the day she told Jerry the reason Bobby was suspicious was because he caught her with another guy several years ago."

T.J. looked at his notes again. "I asked what else he knew about that, but he said that was it. Oh, no. There was one more thing. She told Jerry that the previous guy was a co-worker, but he didn't ask her where she worked."

Jimmy Starbuck moved his body to the edge of his chair. "That's it. I told you I have a feel for these cases. We now know what Bobby Jordan's motive for killing his wife was; and we know that he didn't want to tell us about his wife running around on him. Thompson will have to take the murder charge now.

Lieutenant, you want me to go back over to the D.A.'s office and get a warrant?"

As the lieutenant considered this new information before answering, T.J. spoke. "Don't you think we ought to dig a little deeper before filing charges? I mean I could go talk to Regina's mother and see if she remembers Regina talking to Jerry that day. She should remember if it happened, since the reason she went along was to make sure Bobby wouldn't have any reason to be suspicious.

"We could also check with the bank where she worked and see if anyone knows about her having an affair there with another employee."

Jimmy Starbuck immediately stood and turned toward T.J.'s chair. "T.J. you're trying to make this case into more than it is. Why do you insist on trying to defend this guy? You went out and got the best evidence we have on him so far, and now you want to discount it. If you're going to work homicides, you're going to have to learn to not second-guess your evidence! How about it, lieutenant? Do you want me to get the warrant?"

The lieutenant looked at Wilson. "What do you think Marcus? You think the salesman was telling the truth? Do you see any reason to look at this thing from other angles?"

T.J. Lawson was sure his partner would have to confess that he didn't go on the interview with T.J., but Marcus Wilson had been around too long for such an admission.

"What I think is that if Jimmy can get the warrant, let's do it. Who knows about a car salesman? If his lips are moving, he may be lying, but if the D.A. will take the charges, it's his baby then." If nothing else, Wilson had given a skillful answer without being totally untruthful.

"Ok, Jimmy. Give me about an hour on this paperwork and we'll go back and see Bradley V."

The lieutenant rose and stepped from behind the desk as the detectives began to file out.

"Hold on, T.J. I want to talk to you for a minute."

The lieutenant waved his hand toward a chair as if inviting the young detective to sit as the other two detectives walked out and shut the door. "I just want to tell you that you are going to make a good investigator, T.J. But you have to think of these cases like this. We have to put together enough evidence to charge someone with the crime. All the other follow-up, if the D.A. decides it's needed, like checking with the boyfriend from several years ago, can be handled by the district attorney's investigators before they go to trial. Does that make sense?"

T.J. shifted his body to the edge of the chair. "Lieutenant, I understand what you are saying, but in this case I'm having trouble believing that Bobby Jordan killed his wife. It just seems to me that it would be worth the time to check out everything we can before filing charges. I kinda' like the idea of us pursuing justice; not just clearing cases."

The lieutenant's face began to turn red. "Let me tell you something kid. I've been doing this job for years; Wilson even longer than me. Don't sit there and presume we are just about clearing cases! I admire your enthusiasm. Don't screw it up by getting judgmental about the people you work with." Kellner reached for the door and opened it, inviting, with little subtly, the rookie detective to leave his office.

*****

After they were back at their desks and before T.J. returned, Jimmy asked Wilson, "Did you leave that note from Jenny White on my desk?"

"Yeah, she called Friday afternoon," Wilson responded.

"Well, I don't think there's much to do on that," Jimmy said. "A two year old kid who just lost his mother might say anything." With that Jimmy Starbuck placed the note in his file which he stuffed in a briefcase. He then left the office for a trip to the district attorney's office.

*****

The meeting with D.A. Thompson was quickly completed. Lieutenant Kellner told him about the additional information that had been obtained from the car salesman. Thompson approved the charge of Capital Murder and the two officers left his office with a warrant for the arrest of Bobby Jordan.

Chapter Ten

Upon their return to the homicide office, Jimmy Starbuck and Lieutenant Kellner found Marcus Wilson seated at his cubicle reading a golfing magazine. Kellner advised him that the detectives would serve the murder warrant on Jordan the following morning at the auto parts store where he worked.

"Jimmy, contact Lawson and let him know to be here early in the morning to go with you," Pete Kellner said.

Wilson tossed the magazine on his desk. "Lawson caught a homicide down on the ship channel about an hour ago with Perlman. Lieutenant Dawson asked for a volunteer because Perlman's partner Johnny Bounds is off today. Naturally, T.J. volunteered."

Jimmy Starbuck was quick to respond. "Lieutenant, Wilson and I can handle this. Let T.J. get a little experience with Perlman. He wasn't very excited about closing this case out anyway."

And with that, T.J. Lawson was finished with any official duties on the Regina Jordan murder case.

*****

Tuesday morning Wilson and Starbuck left the office at 8:30 to serve the warrant on Bobby Jordan.

After they were gone for nearly 45 minutes, Pete Kellner picked up the phone, called Jefferson Clay's office and left a message that Bobby Jordan was being arrested for the murder of his wife.

When he returned from the courthouse where he had appeared in a routine matter for another client, Clay read the message and immediately cleared his calendar. He then drove to the police station and attempted to begin the process of making bond for Jordan, but the detectives had not yet placed him in jail.

Clay took the elevator to the third floor where the homicide office was located. He was concerned that after the arrest the detectives might try to interrogate his client before placing him in jail. Upon speaking with Lieutenant Kellner, however, he learned there was no interrogation of Jordan being conducted and that the detectives would have the paperwork available at the jail bonding window in a few minutes.

Two hours later, Bobby Jordan was escorted to the exit door of the bonding office and met by his attorney. As Jefferson Clay drove toward the auto parts store where Bobby's truck was, Bobby told him he was having trouble putting together money to pay him. He would borrow the money to pay for his bond from his sister and her husband. He promised to bring that and the five-thousand retainer to Clay's office later in the day, but he was not hopeful about having more money.

As they drove into the parking lot of George's Independent Auto Supply Store, Jefferson Clay advised Bobby they would discuss it further when they met at his office. Bobby exited Clay's car and walked toward the front door of the store as Clay drove away.

When he entered the auto parts store, the faces of the counter salesmen were solemn. "Hey, Bobby it's good to see you back with us. George is in the office." Gene, the second longest tenured employee, gave a nod of his head toward the office as he spoke. Bobby walked into the office he shared with George Smith.

"Are you ok, Bobby?" George asked.

"I guess I am. Sorry about all the commotion here this morning. My lawyer asked them to call and I would turn myself in, but I guess they wanted to embarrass me." Bobby looked glum.

"Look, Bobby. I hate to do this, but until this is over I can't have you here at the store. The television cameras were all over the parking lot this morning. They came in wanting all of us to comment about your situation. You have got some vacation time and I will pay you for another month, but you're going to need to spend your time with your son and working with your lawyer. I'm sorry." George couldn't look at him. His eyes were diverted to his desk.

Bobby's life had been turned upside down for nearly a week now. He had no reaction to George's decision except to turn and walk out of the office. He waved at the counter salesmen and went to his car.

*****

Upon arrival at his house, Bobby sat at the dining table and reviewed his financial situation. He had little if any equity in the house. He owed more than twenty thousand on Regina's Corvette, and his savings and checking accounts combined held less than seven thousand. He owed Jefferson Clay five thousand for the work on his case and the bond for the murder charge was twenty-five thousand. He had called his brother-in-law Jack Seneca who agreed to place the equity in his home as collateral for the bond money.

Bobby called a realtor and set a meeting for the next morning to list the house for sale. He then looked on the back of the utility room door where he found a set of keys to the Corvette.

Regina's keys were probably still in her purse, which must be in the bedroom, he thought, but he still could not bring himself to enter the room where she had been murdered. He continued to sleep in the guest bedroom and had avoided going into the master bedroom closet by using clothes that were in the utility room, either hung on the door or in the clothes dryer.

He drove the Corvette to a Chevrolet dealership in north Houston. He had considered going to the dealership where he bought it, but the thought of seeing the salesman, Jerry Smith, caused him to decide to drive across town to another dealership.

Bobby had confided in no one of his jealousy when he and Regina bought the car, and later when she took it back to the dealership for service. He knew it was not rational. Smith had done nothing more than utilize a good sales technique of making Regina feel she was special as he was making the deal. He told her how good she would look in the car and that he would like to take a photo to go in the gallery behind his desk of satisfied customers standing beside their new cars.

But Smith didn't know the history. Regina had fallen for a smooth talking banker a few years ago and nearly broke up the marriage. Bobby didn't want to see the salesman again, ever.

He knew that trying to sell the car back to any dealer would mean he was going to take a big loss, but he wanted to get it over with. Bobby would feel some relief if he could just get a handle on his finances and to do that, the car and the house had to go.

At the dealership, the used car manager looked over the Corvette and then went to a computer where he spent five minutes typing and reading something on the screen before returning to the office where Bobby had been invited to wait.

"Nice car," he said. "I can give you twenty-three for it. I don't think you'll get a better offer from a dealer. If you want to sell it yourself, you might get thirty or thirty-two, but if you wanted to sell it yourself you wouldn't be here."

Bobby knew that by tomorrow the dealer would have Regina's Corvette on his used car lot with a price much higher than that, but he didn't care.

"The payoff on my loan should be about twenty 20-K. Tell me what I need to sign and give me a ride back home. It's yours."

Bobby felt good knowing he was making decisions and getting some control of his life. An hour later he was back home with a little more than two thousand dollars added to his defense fund.

Chapter Eleven

When Bobby arrived at Jefferson Clay's office, he learned his brother-in-law had already been there and taken care of the bond. He handed Clay a check for five thousand dollars and was invited to sit in the conference room with his attorney.

"Here's my situation Mr. Clay. I sold my wife's car today and after I paid the loan off, I had about twenty-five hundred left. I am meeting with a real estate agent in the morning to try to sell the house, but I'll be lucky to sell it for enough to pay the mortgage.

"When you dropped me off at work yesterday, George fired me. He said he couldn't have me around the store until the murder charge was cleared up.

"So I've got no job, a two year old son to take care of, a murder charge against me that may send me to prison or worse, and about forty-five hundred bucks in my pocket. You tell me what we do now."

It was the first time Bobby had verbally summarized his personal and financial condition and it did not make him feel good about his prospects.

"No relatives who can help you?" Clay asked.

"I have a brother and a sister. My brother doesn't even own the home he lives in and my sister and her husband just put the equity in their home up for my bond as you know. I wouldn't even consider asking Regina's parents for help and if I did, they couldn't come up with the money I would need." Bobby was feeling the desperation.

"Bobby, I'd like to represent you, but a case like this will take a lot of time. I can't do it for five thousand dollars, unless you want to plead guilty and not fight this thing. Then our goal would be to get something less than the death penalty." Clay sat back in his chair and waited for Bobby to respond.

He suddenly felt as if he was being physically pulled down into deep water in a raging whirlpool. Without realizing it, Bobby held his breath to prevent water from filling his lungs. He became dizzy as he sat across from the lawyer and couldn't move.

"Bobby! Are you alright? Can I get you some water? Put your head down between your knees."

Jefferson Clay was now in front of Bobby and touched his shoulder. The contact caused Bobby to return to the present. He took a deep breath and tried to stand, but the lawyer pressed on his shoulder.

"Don't try to get up just yet, Bobby," Clay said. "Relax for a minute."

A few moments later, Bobby looked at Jefferson Clay and said, "I didn't kill Regina, Mr. Clay. What am I going to do? Is there any kind of financial assistance for someone in my shoes?"

"Bobby, I hate to tell you, but our criminal justice system isn't about justice at all. It's about moving cases through the system so that our political leaders can tell the voters they are tough on crime.

The only way you can get assistance is if you are considered indigent by the court. But to be considered indigent, the Texas courts have held that one test, or the threshold, is that you not be able to make bond. So unless you want your brother-in-law to withdraw the bond, you can't get a court-appointed lawyer." Jefferson Clay returned to his chair behind the desk.

It was more than Bobby could digest. Clay, the only person who Bobby felt was on his side, was now reducing the relationship to money. He understood what the lawyer meant, but it didn't matter. He needed a good attorney. After a few moments Bobby stood and held out his hand.

"Thank you, Mr. Clay for what you have done for me. I guess I will have to ask the court to give me a lawyer, even if it means sitting in jail. I didn't kill my wife and I can't say I did."

Jefferson Clay took Bobby's hand. "Bobby, I'm sorry. I'm going to have my secretary return the check for the retainer. Good luck with this thing."

*****

Bobby drove to Regina's parents' home. When he arrived, both were home and his father-in-law was on the floor playing with B.J.

"I need to talk to the two of you about B.J." Bobby began. "I just left the lawyer's office. Here are my choices. I have enough money to pay the lawyer if I want to plead guilty. If I don't do that my only option is to have the bond withdrawn, go to jail and ask the judge to provide me with a lawyer. No matter what you may think, I didn't kill Regina. I can't tell a judge I did." Bobby took a deep breath.

"I want to know if the two of you will take care of B.J. while I try to work this out. I will give you the money I have, which is about seven thousand dollars, but when that's gone, I won't be able to help until I get out of jail."

Jenny White and her husband Tom looked at each other. Jenny was not sure whether Bobby was telling the truth, but she was suspicious. If Bobby didn't kill their daughter, why did the detective think he was guilty? Who would know better than the detective who was investigating.

"We'll take B.J." Tom said. "When are you going to do this?"

"I'll take B.J. home with me and bring him back with his clothes and some toys in the morning. I know he doesn't understand what is happening, but I want to explain it to him. Please believe me when I tell you that I didn't kill your daughter! It's important." Bobby looked at their faces and knew they were not convinced, although he saw more compassion on Tom's face than he expected.

*****

That night Bobby talked to B.J. for an hour until his son fell asleep beside him. He knew his child understood very little of what he said, but he had to tell him how much he hated being away from him.

The next morning, Bobby placed B.J.'s clothes in a suitcase and gathered most of his favorite toys in a box, both of which he put in the back of his truck. He drove to the Whites' home and took B.J., his toys and clothes to the front door. When Jenny answered the door, Bobby simply picked B.J. up, hugged and kissed him before holding him out for Jenny to take. He turned and walked to his truck with tears in his eyes.

Bobby then returned to his home where he met the real estate agent and filled out the paperwork to list the home for sale. In addition to getting the house on the market, the meeting also took his mind off his son for a little while.

*****

Before going to his lawyer's office the next morning, Bobby sat in his back yard and thought about the past. He had wanted so badly to make his marriage work. Although it had been difficult, he'd forgiven Regina for her affair. He had been trying awfully hard to keep his lack of trust and jealousy in check, but it was all over now. When he finished his coffee he drove to Jefferson Clay's office.

Once there things moved swiftly. Jack Seneca came by and signed the requisite paperwork to have Bobby's bond revoked and Clay accompanied Bobby to the courthouse where, after two hours of shuffling paperwork, Bobby was taken into custody by Harris County jailers. His property was inventoried and his clothing was replaced with an orange jumpsuit. It was nearly eleven o'clock when he was escorted to a large open cell. He entered and heard the cell door slam behind him.

Seven other men were in the large holding cell. Two were lying on the floor and appeared to be passed out. One had obviously urinated while lying in the prone position. His jeans were wet and a small puddle of urine stretched from his crotch nearly to his ankles. Three of the men had staked out areas in three of the four corners of the cell and the other two were leaned against the back wall carrying on a subdued conversation. When Bobby entered, one of the men on the back wall invited him to sit.

"I'm Jack Stark." The man held out his hand. Bobby ignored the offer and sat a few feet away.

"What brings you to our little vacation spot on the bayou?" Jack Stark asked, ignoring Bobby's earlier snub. "You're not drunk and you don't look like a serious crook. Is it child support?"

"Murder," Bobby responded, "and I really don't want to talk about it."

After that exchange no other attempt was made at conversation and within the hour, Bobby was moved to a smaller cell obviously intended to house two inmates, but he was alone in the cell.

Two days later Bobby was taken back to a courtroom where the judge asked him several questions regarding his finances, after which he declared Bobby Jordan to be indigent and advised that legal counsel would be provided for him by the State. When Bobby thanked him, the judge advised that he would be granted a court appointed attorney by the name of John C. Cooksey who would visit Bobby in the jail soon.

THE TRIAL

Chapter Twelve

Bobby sat in his jail cell and attempted to assess his situation for the two days following the appearance in court at which he was appointed legal counsel. Although he no longer had the services of a high-powered lawyer such as Jefferson Clay, did it really matter? This is the United States. Justice would prevail. He didn't need a high dollar lawyer. He wasn't guilty.

Just after noon on the fourth day as a Harris County inmate, a jailer came to Bobby's cell and told him he had a visitor. He was escorted to a row of small cells, each slightly larger than a clothes closet. The jailer opened one of the doors and Bobby entered. As the door slammed shut behind him, Bobby found himself facing a thick glass window that was marred with scratches and smudges. There was a slight human odor in the room and Bobby wondered if the conversations that took place in this room caused the occupants to break into a sweat.

On the other side of the window sat a man who appeared to be about sixty years old with thinning grey hair. He was slightly overweight and dressed as if he had just gone on a shopping spree at the local Goodwill Store. His appearance did not instill confidence.

"I'm John Cooksey and I'm the lawyer appointed to represent you in the murder of your wife."

Cooksey's statement sounded as if it had been repeated thousands of times, which, in fact, it had. John Cooksey had been a criminal defense lawyer for more than thirty years. He began as an idealistic, young, liberal lawyer who intended to change the way business was done in the criminal courts of Harris County. Three years into his career he lost his wife to a neighbor, his home to a mortgage company and his car to a local bank when he stopped making payments.

By the fifth year of practicing law he had learned that criminals don't pay lawyers unless the criminals are on the streets committing more crimes. Most of his clients barely had enough money for a small retainer when he took their cases.

A reassessment of his life story caused him to take a job with the district attorney's office as a rookie prosecutor. The pay was less than a rookie cop made while being trained in the Houston Police Academy. Additionally, the officer needed only a high school education and racked up no student loans while pursuing the training to be licensed.

Cooksey did, however, learn an invaluable lesson about the political game at the courthouse. There was a thriving business in criminal defense work if you could get appointments to indigent cases by the criminal court judges. He also learned that the way most lawyers got these appointments was by making sizeable contributions to the judges' campaign coffers during the election cycle.

So John Cooksey had a job with a regular paycheck. Sure, it was only slightly larger each week than that of the assistant manager at the McDonalds around the corner from the courthouse. That's where he splurged once each week on Friday by treating himself to a Big Mac with cheese, a large order of onion rings and a chocolate shake. But it was better than sitting in an office broke and waiting on the next client to come through the door with a retainer so he could pay the rent.

While working as a prosecutor, he learned the invaluable secret of how to get court appointments from the judges. What he lacked was the financial ability to make contributions which might get him enough court appointed cases to make a respectable living should he choose to return to his chosen profession of representing the downtrodden in society.

John Cooksey, however, had been a smart, innovative and calculating young man. He listened closely to courthouse gossip; he joined the Harris County Democratic Lawyers Association and he began making a list of district court judges who might be vulnerable to a challenge during the next election.

In very little time, he identified Herman T. Crawford as just such a judge. Crawford, a judge for over thirty years was rumored to be in the early stages of senility. In addition to his many embarrassing comments from the bench, he had recently begun to fall asleep while conducting jury trials in his courtroom.

The inevitable then occurred because an enterprising young reporter was assigned to report on a highly publicized murder trial being conducted in Judge Crawford's courtroom. Not realizing or maybe just ignoring the potential consequences of taking photographs inside the courtroom, he had boldly snapped a photo of Judge Crawford peacefully and silently snoozing on the bench as a prosecutor made closing arguments in the case.

The photo was on the front page of the next day's edition, after which the young reporter was held in contempt of court by Judge Crawford. The newspaper paid a five thousand dollar fine on behalf of the reporter. But the damage to Judge Crawford's political career was lethal.

John soon learned while attending one of many Democratic lawyers meetings that a young attorney named Rhett Ryder was going to challenge Crawford in the next election. John brazenly picked up the phone, called Ryder and invited him to lunch. He explained to candidate Ryder that while he had no money to commit to the campaign, he would commit 30 hours of elbow grease each week until the election, working for Ryder's campaign.

His investment paid off handsomely. Rhett Ryder beat the old judge convincingly. After Cooksey resigned from the District Attorney's office, Judge Ryder immediately began appointing him to some of the most lucrative cases that passed through his court. In addition to the court appointments, which paid the bills, he began to see his name in the newspaper and on the local television news associated with some of the more newsworthy cases to which he was appointed.

Soon, John was making sizable contributions to Ryder and other judicial candidates, all of which paid off in more court appointments. He had a nice income which allowed him to live comfortably but far from extravagantly.

As any veteran criminal defense lawyer knows, representing run-of-the-mill defendants day after day in the Harris County Court system can become a drag.

Most of the clients are guilty, if not of the crime charged, then other just as serious criminal acts. It grinds even the good, well-meaning attorneys down; most, at some point in their careers, become victims of the system, just as many of their clients are.

That's where John Cooksey was on the day he met Bobby Jordan. Financially comfortable, but cynical about the entire criminal justice process, as well as the clients he represented.

*****

Bobby stared at Cooksey through the thick window. Did this shabbily dressed lawyer expect a reply?

Cooksey cleared his throat and continued. "So I've read your file and visited with Jefferson Clay about your case. From where I sit, your best bet is to cut a deal, maybe a reduction in the charge, do a few years and get on with your life." Cooksey stared through the scratched window at Bobby.

"Mr. Cooksey, I am sitting behind this glass wall today because I refuse to plead guilty to something I didn't do. If your idea of representing me is convincing me to plead guilty, then you picked the wrong client. I won't do that even if I can get out tomorrow."

Bobby wasn't angry. He was simply finished with any discussion of pleading guilty.

"Let's get something straight, Mr. Jordan. I am more than happy to represent you in a full blown trial on the facts of your case. Don't know that I can win, but I'll give it my best, which is more than you'll ever get from most lawyers who hang around this place. Besides, the bigger fight we have on your case with the district attorney, the more billable hours I have for the taxpayers. So what I am saying is, let's do it if you're willing to gamble."

Cooksey had some life after all and Bobby liked it. The two men spent nearly an hour going over the details of his case and life with his wife and son. Bobby told him about the car salesman, about his wife's affair with a fellow bank employee and every detail of his financial situation, including his interest in the monthly poker game. Cooksey ended their meeting by telling Bobby he was going to request funding for an investigator to follow up on all the loose ends.

Chapter Thirteen

After six weeks in the county jail, Bobby thought he was learning a lot about prison culture. Noise! There was always noise in the Harris County Jail; guards yelling, inmates cursing and arguing, large metal doors slamming shut as another rolled open, and loud buzzers going off every time one of the outer doors was rolled open. He first thought he would never get used to it, but after two weeks he had become so accustomed to the noise that it no longer registered in his consciousness.

He talked to several other inmates during meals and recreation time; men who were waiting for their cases to be tried or for their attorney to make a deal with the district attorney they were willing to accept. Some were destined for their second or third trips to the state prison and they knew it.

One man told him he had committed the robbery he was charged with, but his lawyer was playing the district attorney to get as much time in at the county jail before he agreed to plead guilty and face going back to prison. This man, whose name was Johnny Bender, also told Bobby about life as a convict. Although he was sure he would never be sent to prison, Johnny's stories were fascinating.

"When you first get there, kid, just remember this. Keep your mouth shut and always pay attention to what's going on around you," Johnny had said.

"I appreciate the advice, but I won't be going to prison," Bobby replied. "I didn't kill my wife and I will be found not guilty."

"I know lots of guys who say they didn't do the crime, but they are still in the joint doing the time," Johnny replied. "So, just in case it don't work out for you, take my advice. Try to stay away from all the gangs. You'll get hit on early to join the Aryan Brotherhood or one of the others that are for us white guys. Avoid it if you can. They don't offer protection for free. There's always a price to pay. Stay away from the Mexicans and the Blacks too. It's tough to stay unaffiliated, but if you do join, you've accepted the worst of the entire prison culture. "

*****

Finally, John Cooksey gave him the news. His trial would begin on January 7th. There had been several trial date settings, but for a variety of reasons, as the date drew near, the trial had been rescheduled. Cooksey told him this one was for real. The judge wanted the case off his docket. Johnny had been in the county jail for nearly a year.

Early on Monday morning he was moved from the downtown jail to a holding cell in the criminal courts building. John Cooksey arrived with a blue suit, white shirt, and dark tie with black dress shoes for Bobby to wear in the courtroom. He dressed in the holding cell and was soon escorted to the courtroom where the attorneys began selecting jurors.

The assistant district attorney introduced himself to the court as Johnny Remington. He announced that the state would be seeking the death penalty in this case. It was not news to Bobby, nor his attorney, since there had been numerous conversations with the prosecutor before the trial began. It had been made clear this would be tried as a capital murder case.

John Cooksey communicated well with all his clients; Bobby was no exception. As jury selection began, he explained each time he chose to strike a juror and speculated as to why the prosecutor removed certain jurors as well. By mid-morning on Tuesday, a jury was in place and the judge advised both sides that the testimony would begin at one-thirty the same afternoon. Bobby was returned to the holding cell where he was fed a jail house lunch. He was then left alone to count the minutes before the next chapter in his life would begin to unfold.

When the trial began, Bobby was surprised to find that in addition to the prosecutor who had represented the State in the selection of a jury, the District Attorney himself, Bradley Vance Thompson and a veteran assistant, Paul Scarsdale were sitting at the prosecutor's table. Bobby recognized both from having seen them interviewed repeatedly on the evening news about various criminal cases. Scarsdale had been in the courtroom during jury selection with the young prosecutor, Johnny Remington, but the younger attorney had taken the lead.

Johnny leaned to his right and whispered softly to John Cooksey. "Why is the district attorney himself here?"

Cooksey reached for a yellow legal pad on the table before him, took a pen from his shirt pocket and scratched a note, which he shoved to the left so that it was in front of his client. Johnny read the note: be*cause he is convinced he has a strong case and expects to send you to death row. He will use your conviction, along with others, to get re-elected by proving he is tough on crime.*

Reading the note caused Bobby's entire body to experience a hot flash. Perspiration appeared on his forehead and the backs of his hands. Almost immediately he felt a chill and he shuddered visibly as he sat in the chair. It was difficult for him to comprehend that the three men seated at the prosecution table to his right were all there to try to end his life.

Chapter Fourteen

The young prosecutor began by calling the officer who was first to arrive at the Jordan home on the morning of the murder. He then paraded Bobby's former neighbor, Helen Johnson, Detectives Jimmy Starbuck, Marcus Wilson and Lieutenant Pete Kellner to the stand.

It became clear that the district attorney was building a case of circumstantial evidence by re-creating in the jury's mind a picture of Bobby Jordan on the morning of the murder as a cold, calculating killer whose clothing was soaked in blood as he parried with investigators in the living room of his home.

As he cross-examined each witness, John Cooksey did a credible job of muting the testimony of the police officers by asking specific questions about their training in psychology and whether it was sufficient to permit them to determine whether a person was acting in a calculating manner or whether Bobby might simply have been in shock at having found his wife viciously murdered in their home.

Helen Johnson was a more accommodating witness for the defense and testified that the blood on Bobby's clothing on the morning of the murder could have been from his kneeling beside his wife as he made sure she was, in fact, dead. She also testified that she had never witnessed any behavior by the accused that would lead her to believe he was a murderer.

The defense attorney asked each of the officers who were at the scene and were called to testify if they had observed the Houston Oilers sweater in the bedroom, if they had identified to whom it belonged, and if they had collected it as evidence. Each acknowledged seeing the sweater; one of the crime scene technicians testified he had tagged the sweater as evidence.

Detective Starbuck testified that the sweater belonged to Bobby Jordan, but upon further questioning admitted they had not confirmed that it was his, except in the detective's theory, no one else was in the house. He admitted Bobby had denied owning the sweater.

T.J. Lawson was not called by the prosecution. Prior to the trial beginning, the prosecutor provided a number of documents to the defense indicating that Lawson had some involvement in the investigation, but John Cooksey saw no reason to question why he wasn't called. Years of experience trying criminal cases told Cooksey it was not unusual for the prosecution to call only those witnesses who were most intimately involved in a case or those who were the most experienced testifying on the witness stand.

The following morning, the medical examiner was called to the witness stand. He testified in gruesome detail about Regina Jordan's injuries as he showed photos to the jury of the body grossly distorted and lying in the massive pool of blood beside the bed. He also testified he had determined the time of death to be approximately between six-thirty and seven-thirty in the morning.

Other than the probability that the gruesome photos might inflame some of the jurors to want retribution from the guilty person by way of execution, the medical examiner's testimony was not significantly damaging to the defense's case. He did not point the finger at Bobby Jordan. His testimony did, however, take most of the day on Wednesday and the judge adjourned the trial until the following morning after the medical examiner left the witness stand.

On Thursday morning, the prosecution began the day by calling Regina's mother and father. They both appeared to be grief stricken and were sympathetic witnesses for the prosecution.

Though neither of them had any direct knowledge of who killed their daughter, Jenny White told of her daughter's fear that Bobby would accuse her of having an affair with the car salesman at the dealership where they had purchased the Corvette. She also related that Regina had wanted to return to work but Bobby insisted she stay home with their son.

Bobby's frustration grew as he listened to her testimony. He and Regina had never discussed her returning to work! Jenny White was either lying or Regina had said things to her mother that she had never expressed to him.

Although Mr. White's testimony was less damaging, he testified that his wife was often upset after visiting with their daughter. She believed Regina's marriage was deteriorating and that it was because of Bobby's unjustified suspicions his wife was cheating on him.

John Cooksey objected several times during both parents testimony, primarily because their testimony was 'hearsay' and neither of them had any direct knowledge of what the relationship between Bobby and Regina had been. His objections were successful at times, especially with Mr. White, who was merely repeating what his wife had told him about conversations she had with their daughter. Nevertheless, the jury heard a great deal of what the parents of a deceased child had to say, and it all pointed toward an unhappy marriage between the deceased and the defendant.

Finally, the prosecutors called to the stand the car salesman, Jerry Smith. Smith described the sale of a Corvette to Bobby and Regina Jordan as well as his subsequent conversations with Regina about her marriage and the alleged jealousy of her husband. He also told the jury about Regina's revelation that she had met for drinks with a fellow employee a few years before he sold the car to her and Bobby. Jerry Smith adamantly denied that he had any conversations or meetings with Regina away from the dealership when questioned by the defense attorney, John Cooksey. After Smith's testimony the prosecution rested its case.

*****

Cooksey had been successful in requesting the court to approve funds for an investigator to work with him on the Jordan murder case. He had been curious as to why the prosecutor had not subpoenaed Regina's former co-worker to bolster their theory she was murdered by Bobby because of his jealousy. Instead, the prosecutor had depended on Jerry Smith to relate to the jury his conversations with Regina about the former co-worker.

The investigator's first assignment was to identify and locate this witness and he was successful. Bobby Jordan actually identified the man as Roger Jackson, which the investigator confirmed by visiting the bank where both Jackson and Regina had worked. Jackson was no longer employed there, but the investigator located him in New Orleans where he was currently working for a savings and loan operation.

Once he was interviewed, it was apparent why the prosecutor had not called him as a witness. Roger Jackson admitted his relationship with Regina was much more than an after work meeting for drinks. They had carried on an affair for nearly three months before Bobby Jordan confronted Regina and she confessed. Although he was reluctant to testify, Jackson was subpoenaed to appear as a defense witness.

On the witness stand, Jackson admitted the affair and testified Regina had pressured him to leave his wife in order to marry her. When he refused, she called his wife and told her about the affair. He testified that his marriage eventually disintegrated and he blamed Regina for that, but that he had moved on with his life, relocating in New Orleans.

John Cooksey was elated with the testimony. He knew the discovery of why the prosecutor didn't call Roger Jackson as a witness and his having put Jackson on the witness stand, had now introduced to the jury another potential suspect in the murder of Regina Jordan. He would be sure to drive this home to the jury in his closing arguments. Bobby was less enthusiastic, because he had been unaware that Regina was so seriously involved with Roger Jackson and had considered leaving him to marry Jackson.

Several of Bobby's friends were called as character witnesses and most of them were asked about Bobby's interest in watching professional football. Each of them testified Bobby was a passionate fan of the Dallas Cowboys and never saw him wear any sports clothing with a logo except that of the Cowboys. They each testified they believed Bobby loved his wife and son.

Bobby's former boss, George Smith, testified that Bobby Jordan loved his son like no father he had ever known. He also testified he doubted Bobby would have killed his wife, but that he knew beyond all doubt Bobby would have never left his son in a house with the dead body of his mother. But the prosecutors would have none of that speculative testimony and successfully argued to the judge that the testimony be disregarded by the jury.

Late on Friday afternoon, the judge advised closing arguments would begin on Monday morning. Bobby was led back to his cell and mentally replayed all the testimony. He was sure the prosecutors had only made a circumstantial case. He fell asleep that night believing that he would be free within a few days.

Chapter Fifteen

Bobby was learning about the Texas justice system. He learned that in Texas criminal courts, after all the witnesses have been called, the prosecutor and the defense attorney have an opportunity to make closing arguments to the jury. They each attempt to explain why their positions on guilt or innocence is best supported by the evidence and testimony that has been presented.

That sounds fair enough; but there is one other minor detail. After the prosecutor makes his argument and the defense attorney does the same, the prosecutor is allowed a second chance to rebut whatever the defense attorney might have said in his closing argument. Those who believe the last argument leaves a greater impression on the jurors argue this system may not be quite fair to the defendant. But that's the rule in Texas courts and it is how Bobby Jordan and John Cooksey had to play the game.

District Attorney Bradley Vance Thompson entered the courtroom on Monday morning appearing as if he had just stepped off one of the pages of GQ magazine. His black pin stripe suit was sharply pressed and fit as if he had been born to wear it. He wore a pale blue dress shirt and bold red tie. Peeking from the sleeves of the suit at his wrists were shirt sleeves adorned with gold cufflinks engraved with the initials *BVT* on each.

Thompson knew his arguments would be widely reported in the media and that his image would adorn all the television news channels tonight. With a little luck he might even make the front page of the Houston Chronicle tomorrow. He took his seat at the prosecution table and awaited the judge's entry into the courtroom.

The judge entered at precisely nine a.m. and advised the bailiff to bring the jury in. After they were seated, the judge advised the prosecutors to begin with their closing argument.

Thompson rose and strode purposefully to within three feet of the jury box. There he stood, silent for a matter of about 10 seconds, a time that was later described by one reporter as just the right amount of time for the jurors to fully grasp the magnificence of the well-known district attorney's physical appearance.

"Ladies and gentlemen, I won't bore you with a long closing argument. You have heard the testimony have been presented with the evidence. The judge will give you instructions before you leave the courtroom which will include the standard by which you will determine the guilt of this defendant."

Thompson pointed over his shoulder at the defense table. "Just remember that the standard is not beyond doubt, not beyond a shadow of a doubt or any other standard beyond reasonable doubt. It is clear the prosecution has met that standard in presenting this case to you. Let me summarize.

First, you have the motive. Bobby Jordan was a jealous husband who believed his wife was having an affair with a car salesman. His mother-in-law told you he was so angry and distrustful that he would not allow Regina to return to work as she wanted to."

Holding up two fingers, the Thompson continued. "Second, he had the opportunity. There is no doubt, and it is undisputed by the defense, that Bobby Jordan was at the murder scene only minutes before the murder occurred and within minutes, maybe even seconds, after it was completed. His attorney, Mr. Cooksey, would have you believe he left his home; the intruder came in, brutally murdered his wife in a few short minutes, and then Bobby Jordan returned. Doesn't sound plausible to me, how about you?

"And finally, we have the evidence. All of the physical evidence points to the defendant, Bobby Jordan. The murder weapon belonged to him. No fingerprints at the crime scene but for his and those of the deceased. No evidence of forced entry into the home.

"We top all that off with the fact that the detectives testified Jordan was not the most cooperative of witnesses and we have our murderer. Ladies and gentlemen, unfortunately, as in many murder cases, we didn't have a witness we could bring into the courtroom so that you could see that witness point to Bobby Jordan and whose voice you could hear say that he or she saw Bobby Jordan murder his wife. But what you do have is an accumulation of motive, opportunity and physical evidence, which, together, are nearly as good as an eye-witness; some would say even better! Please help me as I continue to make Houston a safer place to live and find Bobby Jordan guilty of the murder of his wife."

With that, Bradley Vance Thompson turned from the jury, strode to his chair and sat, looking solemnly at the papers on the desk before him.

"Mr. Cooksey." The judge looked down at the defense table.

John Cooksey, looking much as he had the first time Bobby Jordan met him, with a lock of hair askew across his forehead, tie loosely knotted at his neck and a suit that needed pressing, stood and walked to the jury box.

"I've been trying criminal cases in Harris County for many years," Cooksey began. "I have defended innocent men just like Bobby Jordan and I have prosecuted murderers when I worked as a prosecutor. In all those years I never saw a prosecution based so solely on speculation as is this persecution of my client.

"As you have heard several times already and you will again later today, the standard for conviction is beyond a reasonable doubt. It is your decision to make, but what I ask you to remember when you retire to deliberations is that if there is even a scintilla of doubt in your mind and if you are a reasonable person, then you must find my client not guilty.

"I want to bring your attention to several items of evidence and testimony that were glaringly missing from Mr. Thompson's prosecution of this case. Each of these items creates more than reasonable doubt as to the guilt of my client. In fact, together they create a real question as to the competency of this police investigation and subsequent pursuit of the case by Mr. Thompson's office. When you retire to deliberate my client's innocence, please, remember each of these issues."

John Cooksey placed his hand on the rail that ran the length of the jury box. He smiled and made eye contact with each of the jurors before proceeding.

"Let's start with the Houston Oilers sweater that was found in the bedroom at the crime scene. You have testimony from defense witnesses that Bobby Jordan was not an Oilers fan and never wore such a sweater. All you have from the prosecution is the testimony of Detective Starbuck who told you it must belong to my client because it was in his home. Is that what we expect from our crime fighters? They didn't investigate! They just made assumptions.

"The detectives never tried to determine if the sweater could have belonged to the real murderer. Did you notice they didn't present testimony that they attempted to get fingerprints from the sweater. They also didn't tell you about the newest scientific crime fighting tool, which is the collection of DNA from the scene of the crime. That's because they didn't do DNA testing either.

"Let's talk about motive for a few minutes. Mr. Thompson would have you believe Bobby murdered his wife because he was jealous after she had an affair several years ago with a man named Roger Jackson. Did it strike you as curious, as it did me, that the prosecutor did not call Mr. Jackson to testify? Instead a car salesman who barely knew the Jordan family was called to testify about the affair, which occurred long before he even met Regina Jordan.

But you did get an opportunity to hear from Mr. Jackson, because even though it pained my client greatly to sit in that chair and listen to the story about his deceased wife's betrayal of their wedding vows,

Bobby Jordan wanted you to hear what Jackson had to say. He wanted you to know the truth!

Mr. Jackson told you that Regina Jordan ruined his marriage and he blamed her for the disruption in his life. He also testified that he moved from Houston to New Orleans. Does this sound like a man who may have had a REAL motive for killing Regina Jordan? It does to me, too. But as you saw, the police and district attorney ignored this obvious line of investigation. As far as we know, they never talked to Jackson, never considered him a possible suspect and never allowed the investigation to take any turn away from Bobby Jordan as the murderer, even with all these questions that should have been answered."

John Cooksey walked back to the table where Bobby sat. He turned and addressed the jury as he stood beside his client. "Mr. Thompson made quite a show of having witnesses tell you about Bobby Jordan being 'covered with blood'. Remember, he had the officers tell you about his appearance on the morning of the murder. Now, you'll recall that Helen Johnson, the neighbor who watched B.J. on the morning of the murder, testified that she believed the blood she saw on Bobby's clothing could have been there because when he found his wife dead beside their bed, he knelt to see if she was still alive. That sounds perfectly reasonable to me and it should to you as well.

"But here's a more important fact. Bobby went to work that morning dressed in the same clothes he was wearing when the cops got to the scene. Don't you think if he had shown up at work as bloody as the officers testified that he was, his co-workers would have told us that when they testified? Did you want to hear his co-workers confirm that he came to work with blood on his clothing? The prosecutor would have you believe that somehow all the people who saw my client before he returned to his home that morning didn't notice that he was 'bathed in blood' as I believe Detective Starbuck described in his testimony."

The defense lawyer reached out and placed his hand over Bobby Jordan's on the table. He patted Bobby's hand twice then walked back to the jury box.

"My colleagues; I call you that, by the way, because we are here for the same purpose. We are here to see that justice is served. As you begin to deliberate the future of B.J. Jordan's father and whether he will be there for his young son who has already lost a mother, remember this. Neither Bobby nor I had to prove anything last week during this trial. That job fell to the prosecutor and I submit to you that Mr. Thompson failed miserably. If there was ever a case where reasonable doubt existed, this is it.

We beg you! Go into that jury room and exact justice by finding, as I have, that Bobby Jordan is not guilty of the crime of murder or of any other crime. Send him home to raise his son and try to overcome this tragedy. Thank you."

*****

"Mr. Thompson. You may begin your rebuttal." The judge nodded to Bradley Vance Thompson.

The prosecutor stood behind the prosecution table. "Jurors, I will keep this short. As to the great mystery Mr. Cooksey attempted to create regarding the Houston Oilers sweater, let me speculate that there are many Cowboy fans in Houston who also have just a tiny bit of allegiance to our home town football team. You no doubt noticed that although Mr. Cooksey wants you to believe Roger Jackson, a man who lives hundreds of miles east of Houston in New Orleans committed this murder; he didn't argue that the sweater belonged to Mr. Jackson. So what he made was an argument of convenience. If the sweater had the New Orleans Saints logo, no doubt it would have been more convenient to argue it was Mr. Jackson's.

The defense also raised the question of why we did not put Mr. Jackson on the witness stand. Well, that might be a legitimate question but for one obvious fact. Mr. Cooksey DID put him on the witness stand and Mr. Jackson confirmed the prosecution's previous witness testimony that the motive was infidelity.

Lastly, when did the shirt become bloody? Simple answer is, when Bobby Jordan murdered his wife! The medical examiner testified that the death occurred sometime between six-thirty and seven-thirty that morning. Whether the defendant murdered his wife and then drove to work or murdered her after his return that morning, it fits easily within the time of death designated by testimony.

What doesn't make sense is that someone entered the home after Jordan left at six-forty-five, committed this brutal murder and was gone without a trace thirty to forty minutes later when Jordan returned. If you buy Mr. Cooksey's theory, the murderer also somehow managed to break into the Jordan home without causing any damage to a single door or window. While I applaud his attempt to help his client escape justice, the facts just don't support his argument. Justice for Regina Jordan is now in your hands, ladies and gentlemen."

Chapter Sixteen

The judge had the bailiff escort the jury to a room behind the courtroom where they began their deliberations. It was nearly eleven a.m. when Bobby was returned to the holding cell. John Cooksey had made arrangements with the jail personnel who handled courtroom prisoners to have pizza delivered there. He joined Bobby to have lunch and begin the wait for news that the jury had reached a decision.

As they ate pizza the attorney began talking to Bobby. "This is the difficult part of a trial. We have done all that we can. How do you feel?"

Bobby finished his first slice of pizza and responded. "John, I've been really optimistic throughout this ordeal because I know I am innocent. But when the judge sent the jury out of the courtroom to begin deliberations, I realized I am one of only two persons alive who knows absolutely that I did not kill Regina. I just don't know what they may decide."

"Well, let's keep thinking positively," John Cooksey replied. "We did everything we could."

"John, the day I met you I worried I was getting a lawyer whose heart wouldn't be in the job of representing me. I want you to know that no matter what the jury decides I believe you did everything you could. Thanks for your work." Bobby pushed the box of pizza away and sat back in his chair.

At three o'clock Cooksey told Bobby he expected the jury might not reach a verdict before the end of the day. If that happened, he would go to his office early in the morning and wait there for word that the jury had reached a verdict.

At seven o'clock that evening a jailer stepped into the room. He advised them the judge had released the jury until the next day. John Cooksey left and Bobby was escorted back to the jail for another night of waiting.

He was moved back to the courthouse the following morning. He waited again in the holding cell outside the courtroom until ten-thirty when the jailer came to escort him back to face the jury.

"The jury has a verdict," he told Bobby. "Let's go."

*****

In the courtroom John Cooksey was seated at the table. The district attorney and both his assistants were also seated at the table beside Cooksey.

"Ladies and gentlemen, I will be instructing that the jury be brought into the courtroom shortly. They have advised me they have reached a verdict. I caution everyone that I will not tolerate any outbursts at all when the verdict is read." The judge nodded at the bailiff to bring the jury in.

*****

As the jurors entered the courtroom, Bobby looked into the face of each person, hoping to see some indication that he, like each of them, would walk out of the courtroom today a free man.   But he saw no indication at all.   Only two of the jurors made eye contact with him and in both cases it was brief.   The conversation was just as he had seen in movies.

Judge: "Do you have a verdict?"

Jury Foreman: "Yes, your Honor, we do."

Judge: "Bailiff."

The judge, with a nod of his head toward the jury, indicated that the bailiff should retrieve the written verdict from the foreman.

The judge read the paper that was handed him by the bailiff and then handed it back.   The bailiff returned the paper to the jury foreman.

Judge: "Mr. Foreman, what say the jury?"

Jury Foreman: "Guilty, your honor."

*****

Bobby Jordan showed little outward reaction. John Cooksey placed his hand on Bobby's and sat motionless. The judge polled each juror, asking each if this was his or her verdict.   The response was unanimous.

"We will begin the punishment phase of this trial at 1:00 o'clock. Court is in recess." The judge rose and left the courtroom.

*****

The punishment portion of the trial moved swiftly. Though the prosecutor had asked for the death penalty, it was as if Bradley Vance Thompson knew his jury. He called a psychiatrist who testified that Bobby might be a continued risk to society. A lady from the

Criminal Records Division of the Harris County District Clerk's office testified that Bobby Jordan had a previous criminal history. John Cooksey elicited testimony from the Clerk that the offense was minor and had occurred when Bobby was seventeen years old.

John Cooksey also called friends and relatives who testified that Bobby was not a violent person, that they would be comfortable with his watching their children and that he would not be a danger to society.

The two attorneys made their arguments to the jury in short order and the jury retired to begin deliberations on punishment the following morning.

On Wednesday morning, shortly before nine a.m. the jurors began. They advised the bailiff they had reached a decision at nine-twenty-five, less than thirty minutes after they began deliberation. Back in the courtroom, Bobby was sentenced to life in prison for the murder of his wife, Regina.

Several of the jurors agreed to talk with the attorneys after they were dismissed by the judge. A conference room was made available for that purpose. The jurors, answering the lawyers' questions, agreed there was some concern about the prosecution's case, but it weighed heavily that there were no other fingerprints, no forced entry into the home, and that the defense had not elicited more testimony or evidence about who murdered Regina Jordan if her husband didn't commit the murder.

Five jurors agreed they would have voted for acquittal if the death penalty had been their only option for punishment. There was presumption by the lawyers that a deal between the jurors had been reached during the guilt or innocence decision to reject the death penalty. This, if accurate, explained the quick decision on punishment by the jury.

Everyone resumed their lives by noon that day except Bobby Jordan. He would begin a new life with experiences he had never anticipated.

Prison

Chapter Seventeen

As he sat in the chair beside John Cooksey shortly after he was sentenced to life in prison, Bobby Jordan was without emotion. It wasn't that he was resigned to the life that had just been thrust upon him, but that he no longer had any control over what his life would be and he knew it.

No more planning for his defense. There was nothing left to plan regarding being reunited with his son, B.J. Life, as he would have envisioned it for as long as he could remember, was over.

"Bobby, I'm sorry that it didn't turn out better. You know there are appeals that can be made to try to overturn this verdict. But you have to weigh that against the fact that you didn't get the death penalty." John Cooksey placed his hand on Bobby's shoulder.

"I know today is not the time to talk about where you go from here. They will move you to Huntsville tomorrow and you will spend the better part of a week being processed into the prison system. There will be psychological interviews, classification as to what level of risk you will be as an inmate and assignment to a prison unit. I'll contact you in a couple of weeks."

The lawyer rose, gathered his file, patted Bobby's shoulder again and walked from the courtroom with shoulders that seemed to sag with the weight of the day's events.

The jailer had given them a few minutes to talk, but as soon as Cooksey reached the door, he moved toward Bobby and told him to stand. When Bobby complied the jailer placed handcuffs on one wrist and pulled both arms behind his back before shackling the other. He was taken to a holding cell in the courthouse to await transportation back to county jail.

Within the hour, two jailers came to his cell and escorted him to the van that had been used to transport him back and forth to the courthouse. Once back at the jail he was taken to the same cell he had been in since the trial began.

The younger of the two jailers spoke as he backed out of the cell. "Ok, Jordan. Be up and ready to go by five in the morning. You'll be catching the first chain tomorrow."

"I'll be what?" Bobby asked.

"Catching the chain," the jailer responded. "You'll be chained to...," he looked down at a sheet he had in his hand, "to four other boys headed to Huntsville and loaded in a bus. It's called catching the chain. You're going to learn a whole new vocabulary soon." Both jailers walked away.

*****

When he was alone Bobby Jordan sat on the side of his cot and tried to understand what was happening to him. In a few minutes he came to the conclusion that he was mentally and emotionally exhausted and unable to think rationally. So he resorted to a routine he hadn't engaged in for several years. He began exercising.

Within the confines of his cell he began by doing push-ups. He was surprised to find that he could only complete ten. When last he exercised on a regular routine, he would complete three sets of fifty push-ups every other day.

After the ten push-ups, he lay on the cot and completed twenty-five sit-ups. The mattress on the cot was thin and hard. It was perfect for his sit-up exercise. He went back to push-ups and alternated the exercises for five sets of each. Dinner, to use the term loosely, was served to him in the cell after which he again completed five sets of each of the exercises. At nine o'clock he lay on the cot and was soon asleep.

Surprisingly, he slept soundly until about four in the morning. He knew it was close to four because he was awakened by the banging and clanking sounds of guards wheeling large carts with breakfast trays into the run of cells.

Bobby was soon escorted to the basement of the building with four other inmates. Two were Anglo and one of them had obviously been on this bus ride before. He had cheap, narrow, thin blue-lined tattoos on both arms and his neck. He could have been thirty years old or he might have been fifty. The skin on his face looked like leather, but not from too much sun or wind. Like his teeth, all of which were a sickly greyish brown color, his skin and complexion were suffering the influence of the use of methamphetamine drugs.

The other Anglo prisoner was a little older than Bobby, probably forty-five. One of the other two was a large black man who had a defiant and murderous stare and the last was a young Hispanic who looked as if he was not yet out of his teens, but whose body was covered with the same cheap tattoos as the older prisoner.

The five prisoners were shackled together as the jailer passed a heavy chain through a ring in each of the short chains attached to and separating the cuff on each wrist of the prisoners. They were then instructed to sit on a concrete bench against the back wall of the small room.

Bobby's breathing had become shallow and that familiar bitter taste permeated the back of his tongue. He glanced back at the door they had entered the room through. As he turned his head, he noticed a larger metal door with a locking mechanism similar to the locks on the cell doors. Although he had become used to living in a jail cell, the confinement seemed to press in on his body.

Nearly two hours later, there was a buzzing sound outside the large door and it began to slowly slide open. Two more guards walked through the door, wearing the same uniforms as the Harris County jailers he had become so accustomed to. These two would transport the prisoners to Huntsville where they would be turned over to the state prison system.

"Everybody up. We're loadin'," bellowed the larger of the two guards.

The chained inmates stood on command. When the guard who had given the instruction turned and walked out the door, the inmates shuffled along behind him, followed by the second guard.

They walked into what appeared to be a covered parking area. There was a large van with heavy mesh wire on all the windows parked adjacent to the door they had walked through. The door to the van was open. With some difficulty, the five men maneuvered the chains and shuffled to the back of the van.

Bobby was at the end of the chain in the back. Three of the inmates sat on the bench on the driver's side, leaving the last two to sit across from them. The chain lay on the floor in the aisle. Bobby's seatmate was the Anglo prisoner who appeared to be a few years older.

After the prisoners were seated, the larger of the guards sat in the driver's seat and the other walked past the prisoners to a small area behind them and locked himself into a wire cage at the back of the bus. The bus pulled out onto the street and within minutes they were on Interstate 45, headed north toward Huntsville.

*****

"Pardon me, Boss! We makin' any stops between here and Huntsville?" the grey-complexioned prisoner asked from across the aisle.

"We don't discuss our travel arrangements with convicts." The guard's reply was curt as he sat behind the wire of the cage.

Bobby knew that he was now a sub-class of human being. It was evident in the guard's voice and his response. There was clearly a different attitude than he had experienced while in the county jail. He looked straight ahead and made no attempt at conversation.

The inmate next to him finally asked, "This your first time down?"

"You mean my first time to prison?" Bobby looked at his seat mate.

"Yeah, and I think that answers my question. I'm Rackley and this is my second ride."

"Bobby Jordan. How long were you in the first time?" Bobby turned and looked ahead.

He remembered the advice the jail inmate had given him to keep his mouth shut and his eyes open, but Rackley had drawn him out within the first five minutes.

"I did four last time around and I was out for about for a year. I'm down for ten this time," Rackley responded.

Bobby concentrated on the road ahead and tried to avoid creating more conversation. He needed time to figure out how he was going to survive in prison; the best clue he had so far was to keep his mouth shut.

The remainder of the ride was uneventful. Bobby's seatmate didn't initiate any further conversation. The other prisoners were lost in their own private thoughts as well.

Chapter Eighteen

The bus exited the freeway just north of Huntsville and after a few turns and twists was on a narrow, rural road, often referred to in Texas as a farm to market road. A few minutes later the van turned into a long drive toward what was clearly a prison complex. The bus continued down the road that ran beside a high chain link fence with concertina wire bordering the top of the enclosure.

After a right turn, the bus faced a large rolling gate made of the same heavy wire as the fence. There was a sign beside the gate with the words Texas Department of Corrections Diagnostic Unit printed in large block letters. The gate began rolling open as if on cue and the bus passed through. The gate rolled shut; Bobby could see a similar gate directly in front of the van.

Three guards in grey uniforms approached the van. The driver opened the van's door and one of the grey uniforms stepped in and began talking to the driver. The other two grey-suited guards walked around the van, one holding a rod with a mirror on one end, passing it along the undercarriage of the vehicle. The inmates were then unchained and searched by the new guards whose uniforms had shoulder patches indicating they were with the Texas Department of Corrections. A few minutes later the second gate rolled open, allowing the van to proceed through.

Two hundred feet inside the fence the bus came to a stop at a building that appeared similar to a large ranch style home built in the 1950's. The driver shut off the engine; the guard in the back of the bus instructed the inmates to stand in the aisle.

Once every prisoner was on his feet, the driver turned. "Alright, move it along." The driver exited the bus first followed by the inmates.

*****

The inmates were left standing in a large waiting area. A few minutes later several guards, in uniforms similar to those who had met the bus, escorted them through a large metal door.

Once in the next room, they were told to strip and place the jumpsuits from Harris County in a large laundry bag. They were then moved into a shower where they cleaned themselves; each with a rough, non-scented bar of soap. After the shower each was handed a towel, white prison pants and shirt with "INMATE" stamped on the back of the shirt.

The next stop was for fingerprints and a photo. When Bobby was through with the finger printing, he was handed a small board with removable letters. It read TDCJ #02561126; a number that Bobby wouldn't forget for the rest of his life. He sat before a large camera on a tripod and held the board an inch under his chin for the photo.

After all the inmates who arrived with him were printed and photographed, they were taken as a group to a cafeteria in the same building. As they walked through the serving line, they were served by other inmates. The fare was simple; a thin pork chop with rice and beans. All three were slapped onto the tray without comment. Upon reaching the end of the serving line, inmates could pour a paper cup of room-temperature water to drink with the meal.

Twenty minutes after sitting at the large inmate dining table, the guards began demanding that the inmates dispose of their trays and form a line. Minutes later they were in another large room-like area, standing and waiting to be escorted to the next procedure.

When Bobby was taken from the common area into one of several small rooms along one wall, he observed that it appeared similar to a doctor's examination room. There was an older inmate in the room mopping the floor.

"Have a seat," the inmate said dryly, pointing to the exam table in the middle of the room.

Bobby sat on the edge of the table. He didn't care about the advice he had followed so closely since speaking to his seatmate on the bus. He needed to talk to someone.

"Can you tell me how long I'll be at this prison?" Bobby looked at the inmate whose eyes never met his.

"This your first time down?" the inmate asked, although he knew the answer.

"It is and I'd kinda' like to know what to expect," Bobby replied.

"Well, the best advice I can give you is, expect to do what you're told." Bobby was annoyed by the answer but didn't respond.

"What are you in for kid?" the inmate continued.

"I was convicted of murdering my wife, but I didn't do it," Bobby replied quickly.

The inmate finally looked at Bobby. He stopped moving the mop across the floor. "Look kid. You're gonna have a lot of new experiences. If you were ever in the military you know what 'hurry up and wait' means, but the military can't hold a candle to what you'll see here. When that judge convicted you, you lost your time. It belongs to the State of Texas now and you'll spend a lot of it just waiting on the man.

"Only time the boss gets in a hurry around here is when your day starts and when you take the first bite of a meal, no matter what meal." The old inmate seemed to enjoy talking.

"So you'll be here at the Diagnostic unit for at least a week, maybe a little longer. You'll have a physical whenever the doc decides to come in and look up your ass. Then you'll have an eye exam and they'll look at your teeth. Sometime in the next few days you'll have to tell a quack about yourself; how you grew up, what you're mad about, all the stuff you used to think was private. Then they'll decide where to send you and you'll be gone."

"Thanks. My name is Bobby Jordan." Bobby held out his hand and the old inmate ignored it.

"I'm Donnelly," he said as he began mopping again.

"Mr. Donnelly, what am I gonna need to know to survive in here?" Bobby's voice nearly cracked as he spoke. "I've never even thought about being in a place like this and the only thing I know is that a guy in Harris County told me to keep my mouth shut and my eyes open."

"Well, you didn't take that advice very well," Donnelly said, "and it ain't Mr. Donnelly. It's just Donnelly.

"You look to be a little older than most that come in for the first time so you won't have it quite as bad as the younger ones that are on their first ride here, but you can expect this. They're gonna know you're a greenie just by lookin' at you. You're gonna get tested. It might be a chin check or maybe just runnin' a game on you. But whatever it is, you gotta be ready to throw down with whoever it is."

"I don't even understand what you're saying." Bobby expected the doctor to walk in at any moment and he wanted more time with Donnelly. "What's a chin check and runnin' a game?"

"A chin check is when you get punched just to see if you got any fight in you. If it happens, fight hard and don't quit, no matter how scared you are. Once you give up, you'll be somebody's punk because you been put in check. But if they know you won't quit, they'll leave you alone after a while.

"Somebody might wanna give you a smoke or share some of his store. If he does, that's runnin' a game. Nothin's free in here and you'll never quit payin'.

"So the advice you got was good, but it's more than keepin' your mouth shut. It's mannin' up while you're here. Once you get a rep it'll get easier."

Donnelly turned as the door opened; a man dressed in a white smock entered the room. The old inmate put the mop in the mop bucket and rolled it out of the room.

The exam was impersonal with a few questions similar to those a person might get from his personal physician, except there was no bedside manner. The same applied with the dentist and the eye doc as Bobby finished his first day in prison.

*****

The next day was Friday and the routine was much the same as the day before. The new inmates ate breakfast at five that morning and within twenty minutes were shuffled out to a large holding area after which each was taken to a smaller room. There, each was questioned by a psychiatrist about his life history, a psychologist about his experience so far as an inmate, then a social worker recorded educational level and performed other testing related to the intelligence of the inmates.

On Saturday and Sunday the inmates continued the early morning routine, but were assigned various tasks in the cafeteria and laundry room during the day. On Monday, the intake process continued with a short orientation about what to expect once they were assigned and arrived at their various prison units. A visit to the chaplain was offered to those who chose to do so. Bobby declined. He wasn't ready for a jailhouse religious experience.

On Tuesday there was little activity. The inmates were confined to cells after breakfast until late morning, when groups were called out by name to catch a chain to their more permanent assignment on the various prison units. Bobby learned that catching a chain in the prison system didn't include actually being chained to other inmates, but simply being loaded onto a large bus with security windows and guards stationed at the front and the back of the bus.

He had been classified as a medium security risk primarily because of the crime for which he had been convicted. He was assigned to the Wynne Prison Unit which was also in Huntsville, less than four miles from the Diagnostic Prison Unit. Several other inmates had received the same assignment.

Chapter Nineteen

The chain bus arrived at the Wynne Unit just before three o'clock that afternoon. The procedure for the vehicle entering the prison grounds was similar to that Bobby had earlier witnessed when entering the Diagnostic Unit.

Inside the main building, the arriving inmates were segregated by race and told to stand in a line outside a small office. A middle-aged man wearing the military insignia of a major sewn onto a grey uniform similar to that worn by the other guards stepped out of the office.

"I'm Major Tisdale. See that yellow line running along the wall? First rule is stay inside that line anytime you're walking and always walk along the wall on your left." Tisdale looked at a clipboard he was carrying. "Robert Jordan, come with me."

The major stepped to the office door and entered with Bobby behind him. Once the major and Bobby were inside the office, one of the guards who had escorted the white inmates to the hallway, pulled the door shut from outside the office. The major walked around the desk and sat in the overstuffed office chair.

"You are in cellblock B2, cell number 3. Your cellmate is Delbert Matheson. You've got the top bunk.

"I'm sure you've already been told you don't have to work. If you want to work, I will put you in

Industry, specifically you'll be working in the license tag plant. You want to work or not?"

"Yes sir. I'd like that," Bobby answered.

"Alright, in the morning you'll be moved with the rest of the convicts who work in the tag plant to your work assignment. One of the bosses in the hall will take you to your house. Got any questions?" The major was curt and there was no emotion in his voice or his facial expression.

"I don't know of anything to ask." Bobby was becoming anxious because he knew his prison life was about to begin.

The major looked at Bobby briefly and said, "Step out."

When outside the office, one of the guards told Bobby to walk down the hallway. He followed and gave instructions for right and left turns until they faced a set of sliding barred doors, where another guard sat behind a heavy glass window in a small control room that Bobby would soon learn was called a picket.

"New inmate for B2, cell 3," the guard who was directing him yelled as the bars began to slide to the left.

They walked down a narrow hallway with cells on both sides until they came to a cell with the number 3 stenciled above the door. Upon a signal from the guard the cell door rolled open.

"Matheson, this is your new cellmate." The guard turned; as he walked away the door rolled shut again.

There were two cots arranged as bunk beds on one side wall. Delbert Matheson was lying on the bottom bunk. He was an average size man with a pale complexion. He barely glanced at Bobby.

"Your bed," he said, pointing his thumb in the direction of the bed above him. "I been here seven years and don't want any shit from you. You stay out of my way and we'll get along okay. What's your name?"

"I'm Jordan," Bobby said as he surveyed the small room that would now be his home.

"What you here for?" Matheson sounded as curt as the major had.

"They said I killed my wife."

"Where'd they put you to work?" Matheson continued.

"Making license plates." Bobby stretched out on the bed.

"Not a bad job. It's hot and boring, but it beats bein' put in a field squad. I work in the mattress factory."

Bobby didn't ask any questions. He knew he needed to get a feel for things first.

Soon the door began rolling open, someone shouted 'B2, chow time', and Matheson stood. He looked at Bobby and said, "Come on. It's chow time."

The two men were escorted to a larger room with a television in it. This, Bobby learned, was the day room, where the B2 wing of inmates would wait for a signal to be escorted to the cafeteria. Soon they were moved to the cafeteria where they walked through the line and were served beans, rice and a concoction that looked like a poor excuse for hamburger helper. After eating, they returned to their cell.

"If you need something to read, I've got a couple of magazines," Matheson said.

Bobby lay back on his bed and replied, "No thanks." He remembered what the old inmate had told him at the Diagnostic unit.

*****

The next morning after breakfast, Bobby was escorted out to the license plate plant with a large number of other inmates. As when the van had entered the prison property, the inmates passed through one rolling gate where a headcount was performed. A second gate was then rolled open and the inmates passed into a second secure area for a second headcount. After this, the inmates were turned into the tag plant where Bobby and a black inmate, who had been on the bus with him the day before, were met by a tag plant supervisor who introduced himself as Mr. Martin.

Mr. Martin walked Bobby to the end of a machine and demonstrated to Bobby how it would spit out license plates two at a time. There was a stack of empty boxes at the end of the machine and Martin explained to Bobby that his job was to place a sheet of thin paper between each set of plates and place them in a box. When a box was full, Bobby was to record the plate number of the last set on the lid, close the box and set it aside.

He began working immediately. Within thirty minutes he had settled into a routine; he realized that it was a mindless job. The building was hot and there was no air conditioning. There were several windows twenty feet or so above the floor with heavy mesh metal covering the opening. They were cranked open, however, the open windows resulted in very little breeze on the floor where the machines were running.

Late that afternoon Mr. Martin approached Bobby's work station and stood behind him watching him work. "Is this your first time here?" he asked.

"Yes sir."

"Well, I've been watching you today. If you keep working like you have so far, you'll do fine. This is my shop and I don't like drama. So just do your work and we'll get along fine."

*****

Bobby was returned to his cell block; and once again witnessed the routine of rolling doors in order to enter the cellblock, then the cell. He found Matheson reading a magazine as he lay on his bed.

"We eat in about fifteen minutes and you can go to the day-room after that and watch television until nine o'clock. You want a magazine?" Matheson turned his gaze from the magazine he was holding toward Bobby.

"No thanks." Bobby placed his hands behind his head and stared at the ceiling.

"Look, if you think I'm gaming you, don't. I ain't interested in anything but doing my time." Matheson returned his attention to the magazine.

Chapter Twenty

Ten minutes later, the soon to be familiar yell of 'cellblock B2, chow time' was heard again as the cell doors began rolling open and the two cellmates were moved to the day room with the same group of inmates. This time, however, there were black inmates from another block already in the day room.

Bobby stood well inside the room. Most of the chairs were occupied by the inmates from the other cellblock. He leaned his back against the wall and waited.

He concentrated his vision on the television. Almost immediately he sensed that someone had moved from behind him and was standing at his side. He looked to his side to see a muscular black man staring menacingly at him.

"What you doin' standin' in my way, peckerwood?" The man spoke loudly enough so that he could be heard above the noise in the room which subsided slightly.

Bobby quickly took in everything in the room within his peripheral vision without turning his head. The only guard he could see was at the door of the day room and he was talking to someone outside Bobby's line of vision. He slowly moved his body away from the wall.

"Sorry, man. I didn't know." Bobby looked at the inmate and started to walk away.

He knew he was probably facing the defining moment of the rest of his life as a Texas prison inmate. The look on the black inmate's face confirmed it as he grabbed Bobby's left arm, swinging him around, nearly causing him to lose his balance.

Not another word, Bobby thought. He spun and smashed his fist as hard as he could into the black inmate's face. Blood spewed from the man's nose as he slipped and fell. Bobby made his first mistake. He stood over the inmate instead of continuing the fight. Immediately he was grabbed by the leg and pulled to the floor. Bobby was no match for his attacker. In seconds, he was being pummeled in the face.

Moments later four guards were on top of both inmates and the fight was over. The black inmate had a small cut on the bridge of his nose and another on his left nostril. Bobby's nose was broken and swelling. He was bleeding from the left ear and there were cuts above both eyes. He had been beaten by a professional street fighter, but after he was pulled to the floor, he had remembered to never stop swinging.

After an hour in the infirmary, Bobby was taken to a different area of the prison. The guard who escorted him told him that he was going to solitary until a disciplinary hearing was held. He had begun to feel the results of the beating. Then he learned that in solitary his food consisted of bread and water.

Two days later the cell door rolled open. "You got a disciplinary hearing in 10 minutes," the guard said. "Let's go."

Bobby was escorted to an office where a major was seated behind a desk; two other uniformed guards were seated to his right.

"I'm Major Denning and you are here for a disciplinary hearing." The major looked at the file before him. "You attacked Inmate Carl Smith in the Day Room night before last. You have anything to say?"

"He told me I was blocking his view of the television and when I tried to move out of his way he grabbed my arm. I hit him as hard as I could. I don't want any trouble but when I was at the Diagnostic Unit an old inmate named Donnelly told me that if I didn't fight I would be somebody's punk. That's why I hit him."

"Sit down, Jordan." The major nodded toward the chair in front of his desk.

"Smith goes by the name of Jigger. We call him Jigger the Nigger, but you probably shouldn't. For the guy who took the first swing, it looks like you got the worst of the matter. I don't care who blocked whose view of the television and I don't care about whether you end up some nigger's wife in here. I do, however, care about peace and quiet in my day room.

"We need you on the line in the license plant so I'm letting you go back to work. We'll record your two days in solitary as your punishment. Understand this, though. No more problems or you won't like the consequences.

"The nigger, Smith, is being transferred to the Michael Unit in Tennessee Colony. This isn't his first problem. He'll get tuned up while he's at Michael.

"By the way, that was old man Donnelly who gave you the advice. It was worth listenin' to, but Donnelly had to kill a nigger and a white convict to keep from becoming their punks. Hope you don't have to. Now get outta here."

Bobby was returned to his cell for the remainder of the day. When his cellmate, Matheson, came home from working in the mattress factory, he looked at Bobby and grinned.

"Well, I guess everybody knows you don't intend to be no nigger's wife," Matheson said as he stood staring at Bobby.

"You'll have to watch out for a while though. The guy you hit is Jigger. He runs the Bloods here. I doubt you feel like going to the day-room anyway, but probably best to stay away from there 'til things cool down."

Bobby didn't respond. He was depressed. It was clear to him that he would be living like a wild animal as long as he was in this place. He drifted off to sleep after another hour. When he awoke the next morning it was to the now standard 'Cellblock B2, chow time'.

*****

As Bobby was escorted toward the license plant to go to work, he tried to digest what the major had told him about the old man. Could Donnelly, the mild-mannered old man who was old enough to be his grandfather, really have killed two men while in prison?

He went straight to his job boxing plates; two hours later Mr. Martin walked over to where he was working. "I guess you haven't learned how to stay out of trouble. You got one free ride on this deal, but it won't happen again. If you were my son I'd tell you to stay away from the blacks and the Mexicans, don't hook up with the Aryans or any other gang. To do that you need to stay out of the day room and away from the crowd when you're in the rec yard. Spend your time in the library or your cell.

"It's tough in here, but you won't get any sympathy. I hope you make it." Martin walked away.

*****

Days became weeks, which soon became months. Bobby had one more incident when an Aryan Brotherhood leader threatened him after he refused to "ride" with his gang. The convict told him if he tried to stand alone no one would help him when Jigger and his boys got their opportunity. But Bobby stood his ground; soon he was seen as a loner who didn't get involved in anybody's business.

In a stroke of luck for Bobby, word through the prison rumor system came to the Wynne Unit that Jigger was stabbed to death by a member of the Aryan Brotherhood less than a month after being transferred to the Michael Prison Unit. While there was tension with Jigger's former friends, Bobby learned how to avoid them and other groups of gang members for the most part.

John Cooksey visited Bobby three weeks after he was settled in at the Wynne Prison Unit. Bobby was still recovering from the broken nose and had visible scars above his eyes. He told Cooksey of the fight in the day room and that he was not sure he would make it as a prison inmate. They talked about his conviction and a decision was made to go forward with an appeal, challenging the State on a number of legal issues, some of which were standard boilerplate appeals. Cooksey didn't mention how he would be paid. Bobby held little hope of getting out of prison before he was an old man.

Chapter Twenty One

After several months, Bobby took Mr. Martin's advice and inquired about being allowed to visit the inmate law library. There were a limited number of inmates allowed to be in the library at any time; inmates were screened closely to see if they were "writ writers" before being permitted to spend time there.

Bobby learned that a "writ writer" was a convict who continuously prepared hand-written legal appeals for himself and other inmates. After several weeks, he gained permission to visit the library two times each week for two hours each visit. He tried to miss as few of his visits as was possible. He was fascinated by what he read in the library.

The only disappointment regarding his library privileges was that, as with every other aspect of prison life at the Wynne Unit, he had no freedom. He was escorted to work; he was escorted to every meal; and now he learned he would be escorted on every visit to the inmate library and strip-searched upon exiting. The prison system was very serious about not allowing legal material into the hands of writ-writers and other malcontents outside the confines of the library. Bobby could write notes in his own handwriting and take them back to his cell, but he could remove no other written material.

When he had been at the Wynne Unit for a year, he inquired about the prison education program. He learned that he could take college courses offered by

Lee College, which was physically located in Baytown, Texas. The college had classroom space on the second floor of the main building on the Wynne Unit, which also housed the administrative offices.

If he was accepted, he could attend evening courses and if necessary could be "laid-in" for half days during which he would be excused from his work schedule to attend classes. Once he got the information, he applied to the program and was accepted. His first two classes were on Monday and Wednesday evenings. Soon after he began attending the classes, he realized how much he enjoyed being in school and immediately set a goal of achieving a bachelor's degree. To the extent that prison can be routine, Bobby was settling in.

He recalled that John Cooksey had raised the issue of DNA evidence in his closing arguments. One of the first articles he stumbled onto in the library was a review of the first case of the use of DNA in 1986. In that case, a professor at Leicester University in England used DNA technology to prove that a man who had confessed to two murders did not commit the crimes. He learned through further reading that the first ever conviction of a person by using DNA evidence was also in England the following year, when a man was convicted of rape.

Bobby's excitement and interest began to grow. Was it possible that there was a way to prove his innocence through the use of DNA? He could hardly wait for his next trip to the library. Bobby soon learned that DNA had also been accepted by the courts in the U.S. beginning in 1988 when a Virginia man was convicted of murder and shortly afterward when another had his New York conviction overturned based on DNA evidence.

Bobby went to his cell after learning of the cases in Virginia and New York. He couldn't sleep. What about Texas? He had seen no articles about police using DNA in Texas. He knew he had to get back to the library.

It was a week before Bobby entered the library again. There was not a good system to use to do research in the prison library, so he began thumbing through some old law journals. After more than an hour and just before giving up for the night, he opened the pages of a Texas Lawyer publication and found a scrap of yellow paper between the pages that appeared to have been torn from a legal pad. There was handwriting on the paper that simply said, *DNA - find the H. Chronicle article about Bethune.*

Not thinking about being searched as he left the library, Bobby put the scrap of paper in his pocket. When he submitted to the strip search at the exit, he got lucky. A guard who had never seen Bobby before conducted the search and when he turned his pockets inside out before removing his pants, Bobby laid the note on the table in front of the guard as if it was his own. The guard looked at the note and made no comment. The strip search was completed and he returned to his cell with the note tucked safely in his pocket.

Chapter Twenty Two

Two years after arriving at the Wynne Unit, Bobby Jordan was well on his way to getting an associate degree through the prison education program. He still enjoyed pursuing this goal and had begun taking some classes during the day. As a result, he was scheduled to miss work two half days each week.

He took a freshman English class from Ms. Halliday. After completing that class, at each new semester he looked for her classes and tried to enroll in at least one. Ms. Halliday taught English, writing and public speaking classes. Her physical appearance reminded him of Regina; sometimes he dared to trigger that part of his mind that wanted to remember. There were some physical similarities, the softly tanned skin, sun-streaked light brown hair, and brown eyes framed in thick black lashes. She was about the same height as Regina, and appeared to have a nice slender, well-toned body. Sitting in her class, he thought of Regina.

Bobby had been proud of Regina's appearance. She had kept her lovely, athletic shape even after B.J. was born. He recalled her telling him that, as a child, she had been somewhat of a tomboy, playing softball, volleyball and tennis. She'd taken gymnastics and made the cheerleader team in high school. He used to wonder how they had ended up together. He'd always admired her in school. But they ran in different social crowds. They hadn't dated until he'd returned from military service and his sister picked him up from the airport. On the drive home, they'd stopped by her bank. Regina was working there, and recognized him. It was the first time she seemed to take an interest in him.

His thoughts were crossing that line. He wouldn't go there. Bobby forcibly refocused his attention on Ms. Halliday's lecture. Like Mr. Martin, she seemed to have a different view of convicts. She did not seem to care who her students were, but only whether they succeeded in her classes.

Every inmate who had been in the system for any time at all knew that if a guard, teacher or any other employee became too familiar or open with an inmate they probably would jeopardize their employment with the prison system. The more manipulative inmates intentionally flirted and tried to engage the female employees, some of whom were easy prey for the affections of a convict skilled in the art of such manipulation. Usually the intent was to nurture a relationship that might result in the employee bringing contraband into the prison unit or to engage in a sexual relationship. There was a thriving drug trade in the prison system and often these employees became the mules delivering the product.

Ms. Halliday was not one of those employees. She set boundaries with inmates. On two occasions, Bobby had witnessed inmates expelled from her class who inappropriately attempted to foster a more personal relationship. Bobby thought her classroom facial expression was best described as serious. He dreamed of a day when he might talk to her in an atmosphere where his intentions would not be suspect, but he resisted all temptation to engage her in a personal conversation.

His mind wandered again, and he caught himself wondering if it was Ms. Halliday's attitude that really reminded him of Regina. He remembered times when he used to tease her and call her "Regal Regina" because of the serious look on her face. Sometimes "the look" could be misinterpreted as being haughty by those who didn't know her well.

And those brown eyes could pierce right though a person when challenged. But sometimes they could be soft, worried, or tearful. Like the time she had told him she had revealed too much about herself to the car salesman who sold them the Corvette.

Regina had then felt guilty and worried because something too close to the truth had just slipped out to a stranger. She and Bobby had been working very hard on rebuilding their marriage and were learning how to safely discuss anything that disturbed one of them. She knew Bobby noticed that the salesman had been a flirt. She had wanted to assure him that her "chaperone" was with her because she hadn't wanted him to ever worry again about anything like that. Her brown eyes had been soft, worried and tearful then.

Bobby realized he had not only crossed that line again, but had opened a door that was unsafe to go through. He closed his own eyes and breathed deeply, willing his mind to close that door.

Bobby wouldn't allow himself to consider the irony that Regina's conversation with the salesman had contributed to his current situation. The car salesman had remembered his perception of events in a manner that tended to justify his own behaviors, beliefs and ego.

*****

He had adjusted to the routine of prison life and was glad he worked for Mr. Martin in the license tag plant. He talked to other convicts who told horror stories about the bosses they worked for, but Mr. Martin was straight up. Occasionally he even offered words of encouragement to Bobby, although he never allowed the relationship to become personal.

*****

John Cooksey visited Bobby twice in those two years; the first being a few weeks after he was processed in; the second time was just after Bobby had found the scrap of paper in the law journal. Cooksey made the trip to see how his client was faring as a prison inmate, but Bobby turned the conversation to his appeal immediately.

He talked briefly about what he had learned about DNA evidence and then he asked, "Mr. Cooksey. Did you ever consider trying to get that Oilers sweater tested for DNA?"

John Cooksey sat back in his chair. "You know, I raised that in my closing arguments, but quite frankly, I didn't consider the possibility of asking the court to allow us to perform the test. As you know, even now, two years after you were convicted, there are still appeals winding their way through the system. Those cases will ultimately determine the role DNA will play in cases such as yours."

Bobby moved on to another matter. "Oh, I need to ask you for another favor." He pulled the note from his pocket. "Can you see about finding a story in the Houston Chronicle about someone named Bethune?" He handed the note to the lawyer.

"What's it about?" John Cooksey studied the note.

"I'm not sure but I found the note while I was looking for stories on DNA. I'd just like to see what the story is. It may be nothing."

John Cooksey was a compassionate man. He looked at Bobby and realized Bobby was researching DNA evidence because he needed hope. Although he was somewhat concerned about helping Bobby build up false hope, he knew he would look for the article.

"If I find it, I'll mail it to you. Is your son visiting you here?"

The lawyer was placing his file back in the expandable folder he had carried in. When he looked up he saw a dark mask of withdrawal had altered Bobby's facial expression.

"His grandparents bring him occasionally, but I'm not sure he really even knows why he comes. I think I've lost that relationship too." Bobby looked down at the table.

One reason John Cooksey didn't visit his clients in prison very often was that it often depressed him when he talked with them about how their lives were affected by being away from family. Seldom did his clients evoke as much compassion as Bobby Jordan did. He left the Wynne Prison Unit that day vowing not to return.

*****

Two weeks after visiting Bobby, Cooksey had a rare afternoon during which he had no client meetings scheduled. He decided to leave the office early and began packing his briefcase. As he straightened his desk, he saw the note Bobby had given him and decided to go to the Houston Chronicle offices and see if he could find anything on the Bethune story.

An hour later he sat in the archives area of the newspaper's massive building and began reading a story that had been printed in November of 1988, more than four years earlier. The article related the story of thirty-two year old Henry Lee Bethune who had been convicted of raping a seventy-four year old woman. During the trial, DNA evidence was introduced by the prosecutor and allowed in as evidence by the judge for the first time in a Harris County court. Other than the novelty of it being the first, Cooksey could not understand his client's interest in the case, but he copied the story and dutifully mailed it to Bobby the next day.

Over the following few weeks he was haunted by Bobby's response to the question regarding his relationship with his son. He also began to consider whether he should have tried to have the Oiler sweater tested, even though the prosecutor had shown no interest in such testing. He knew that before he took on the case, Jefferson Clay represented Bobby briefly. He decided to have a visit with Clay.

Chapter Twenty Three

Jefferson Clay answered the call that his secretary transferred to his office after telling him that John Cooksey was on the phone calling about the Bobby Jordan case.

"John, how are things going for you?" Clay asked as a greeting.

"I'm doing well, Jefferson. I hope things are going the same for you. Listen, I'd like to come by and visit with you for a few minutes about the Jordan case. Do you have time today?" John Cooksey was not a man to procrastinate once he had made a decision.

"Sure, John, my schedule is open pretty much all afternoon. Just come on by the office," Clay replied.

Jefferson Clay was curious as to what might be going on with the Jordan case. He had followed the case through trial and even dropped by the courtroom twice to listen to testimony. It was one of those rare instances in which he really believed a client who denied he committed the crime with which he was charged. He had experienced a twinge of regret that he had not continued with the case when he heard that Jordan was found guilty.

John Cooksey arrived at Clay's law office a few minutes before one p.m. He was met in the reception area by Jefferson Clay who was talking to the receptionist when Cooksey entered. Clay immediately invited him into his office.

"What's up with the Bobby Jordan case, John?" Clay began.

"Well, I just want to get your thoughts on a couple of things. As you know, Jordan was convicted of murdering his wife and is in prison now. We filed some procedural appeals, but there's not much there.

"I've visited him in Huntsville a couple of times and he has become a convict lawyer trying to find out everything he can about DNA evidence.

"I always thought there was a good possibility that he wasn't guilty of killing his wife and thought the district attorney put on a pretty shoddy case, but they convinced the jury." Cooksey paused and gave Clay an opportunity to respond.

"Well, I guess I thought he was innocent from the day he told me that he wouldn't plead guilty no matter how good a deal I could get him and went off to the county jail so he could get a lawyer appointed. Quite frankly, I thought he was pretty lucky that the judge appointed you."

Jefferson Clay still wasn't sure where this conversation was going. But Cooksey didn't let the suspense build for long.

"Jefferson, I'm not so sure he was lucky to have me as his attorney. You know there was a piece of evidence recovered in the room where his wife's body was found that he always said didn't belong to him and it had quite a bit of blood on it. I argued to the jury that the police should have had it tested for DNA, but I didn't know much about DNA evidence at the time and I didn't seriously consider pushing any harder for testing. That may have been a critical mistake." John Cooksey was relieved to have voiced what had been bothering him since his last visit with Bobby Jordan.

Clay responded, "DNA evidence is cutting edge science. It's going to change the entire criminal justice system, John; but when you went to trial on the Jordan case we didn't necessarily see it coming. You know, it had been just a little more than a year since the first case involving DNA was used in our local courts."

Cooksey interrupted, "Yes, I know. Bobby Jordan found an article, or at least a note about an article, in the Houston Chronicle about that case. It was concerning a guy named Bethune. I found the article and mailed it to Bobby.

"At any rate, I haven't spent much time getting up to date on DNA evidence, but I think I am going to try to get that sweater tested. I wanted to talk to you for two reasons.

"First, I guess I needed someone to bare my soul to regarding my misgivings about how I handled the case at trial; and second, I would like to hear your opinion about whether you think trying to get that testing done is worthy of the effort. You know, there's no funding by the State for this kind of representation of a guy who's already been found guilty."

Jefferson Clay leaned back in his chair and placed his hands in front of his face, touching his chin as if he was praying. "Well, I guess I can make a little confession myself, John. You know I don't take court appointments. I've been blessed with a good number of clients over the years with the money to pay well for their defense and they have made me a wealthy man. Bobby Jordan isn't the first client I cut loose at the point they couldn't pay for their defense, but he's the only one that I am absolutely convinced didn't commit his crime. I've felt a little guilt about it for a long time now. You having come here today must have been providence, because it seems to me that it may offer me an opportunity to assuage my guilt.

"Not only do I think the effort is worth it, but I want to help you pursue the testing. Let's hope the evidence is still available. Wouldn't be a surprise to learn the court can't find the evidence, but if they can, let's try to get that man back where he belongs."

John Cooksey was surprised. He had not expected such an offer.

The two lawyers spent the next two hours discussing strategy. They finally concluded that they would file a motion in the district court to have the sweater tested for DNA evidence, based on the fact that the science concerning such evidence had developed dramatically since the trial of Bobby Jordan.

*****

John Cooksey was driving to Huntsville to meet with Bobby Jordan again. He had been depressed after his last visit because Bobby's situation seemed so hopeless. When Bobby had told him he believed his relationship with his son, B.J., was damaged beyond repair because of his prison sentence, he had quietly decided not to visit again.

But today Cooksey would have some good news for Bobby. They would begin the fight to have an analysis performed on the Oilers sweater. Not least of the good news that he would deliver was the addition of Jefferson Clay to the defense team. Cooksey had practiced law for years and rarely got excited about a case, but today was different.

Bobby looked up from the metal table he sat behind when the attorney entered the visitor's room.

In less than three years, he had aged dramatically. John Cooksey thought about how presidents seem to age rapidly while in office. Then he realized the absurdity of his comparison and nodded his head in greeting.

"Did you get that article you asked for?" He began.

"Yes, sir, I got it late last week." Bobby had no enthusiasm in his voice.

"What was important to you about that article?" Cooksey asked.

"It means that Harris County courts have already admitted DNA evidence to be considered in a case such as mine. Now I have to figure how to get someone to listen to me. There should be some kind of DNA evidence on that sweater of the person who owns it. I know my DNA won't be on it, but it makes no difference if I can't get someone to pay attention."

Bobby looked back at the spot on the metal table he had been concentrating on when the attorney had entered the room. He was clearly discouraged.

"Bobby, after I sent you the article I visited with Jefferson Clay. The two of us want to pursue trying to get the DNA evidence considered and your conviction overturned. That's why I'm here today, to get your approval."

Bobby's head snapped up so quickly that John Cooksey thought something had frightened him, but then Bobby frowned and responded to the news. "You know I can't pay for a lawyer and the best I've been able to learn, no court will provide counsel for a case like this. Mr. Clay doesn't work for free and you've probably wasted more time on this case than you should have on the appeals."

"Bobby, neither of us is asking to be paid. We both believe that you are innocent, although as I think back, I'm not sure I have ever told you that.

"I was ready to take the case by myself but wanted to get Jefferson's view about it. I had no idea that he would want to join me, but he says you are the only client he ever had who he is convinced beyond a doubt is innocent. If you want us, we're ready."

Bobby Jordan hadn't cried in a long time, but tears came to his eyes as he sat staring at the lawyer. "I want out of here Mr. Cooksey. I never thought I would have this kind of help. Thank you."

Fighting for
Justice

Chapter Twenty Four

John Cooksey and Jefferson Clay made an appointment with District Attorney Bradley Thompson. Thompson had recently run for and won a seat on the Texas Court of Criminal Appeals. He was serving the remainder of his term as district attorney before becoming one of a select few appellate court justices in Texas.

"How can I help you gentlemen?" Thompson came right to the point as soon as the men were seated in his office.

Clay responded, "We are representing Bobby Jordan. You remember him? He was convicted of murdering his wife."

"Oh, yes. I won't soon forget that trial. I haven't kept up with the appellate work on the case, but I can't imagine there will be a reversal." Thompson looked at the two lawyers expectantly.

"We are preparing to ask for a hearing before the trial court for the purpose of having the court order DNA testing on some of the evidence that was admitted during the trial. We're here because we would like your office to join us in this motion," Cooksey said as he leaned forward in his chair.

"I would have to review the file, but I don't recall any evidence that might mitigate your client's culpability in the murder of his wife. Exactly what evidence might you be referring to that you believe needs to be tested?"

Jefferson Clay glanced at his co-counsel and responded. "We want to test the Houston Oilers sweater that was found in the room where Mrs. Jordan was murdered. As you may recall, our client has consistently maintained the sweater wasn't his. We're sure his DNA won't be found on the sweater and it's possible that the murderer's will be."

Thompson stood behind his desk. "Gentlemen, maybe you should talk to the new district attorney after I leave office in January. My inclination is that not only would I not join you in making such a request of the court, but I would be likely to vigorously oppose such a motion. In my estimation, it would prove nothing, but maybe Paul will have a different view. You both know Paul Scarsdale, I assume. He's a good man. I'm sure he'll do a great job in this office when I am gone."

"Yes, we know him and if necessary we'll visit with him, but I'm disappointed that you won't join us in this effort. It is really what our entire justice system is about. It's about seeking real justice not just a high conviction rate."

John Cooksey surprised even himself with the tone of his response. He was more than a little irritated that Thompson wouldn't help them.

Jefferson Clay, however, was not about to offend a man who would soon be sitting on the criminal appeals court, which, in Texas, is the equivalent of the State Supreme Court for criminal matters.

"Judge, we appreciate your forthrightness. We'll visit with Scarsdale. Thank you for your time."

With that Clay rose from his chair followed by his co-counsel and they left the district attorney's office. Outside the office Cooksey stopped. "Jefferson, I apologize. That self-righteous political hack has no conscience, but I shouldn't have insulted him."

"Don't worry about it. No harm done. Let's see if Scarsdale is in his office." Clay put his hand on Cooksey's shoulder as he spoke.

Paul Scarsdale had an office just a few feet from Thompson's office. The two men walked in hoping that they might be able to see him before they left the building and they were lucky.

They entered his office and got exactly the same response from the soon to be district attorney they received from the current one. John Cooksey managed to mask his frustration better than he had in Thompson's office and the two men left the building.

Having prepared the motion before visiting with the district attorney, the next step was to file it with the court, which Cooksey did after he and Clay separated. They would have a hearing within two weeks.

*****

When the date of the hearing arrived, it was a non-event. A young assistant district attorney appeared in court and asked for a postponement until after January in order that the new District Attorney, who would take office on January 1, might have an opportunity to develop a position regarding the motion to perform DNA testing. Of course, Clay and Cooksey knew the soon to be district attorney already had a position on the DNA testing they were requesting, but they also knew that justice in Texas often moves at the same speed as a Central American sloth. The judge granted the state's motion and a hearing was set for the following March.

In the interim, both Clay and Cooksey began to sink their teeth into the Jordan case. Clay reviewed his file on the case and then began the arduous process of reviewing the trial transcript. At the same time, John Cooksey decided to look back over the State's witness list and try to find some evidence that might be used in the attempt to test the sweater.

Just before Christmas, the two lawyers met again to discuss their progress. "Let's try to talk with some of the people who were involved in the investigation." Clay suggested. "I would like to know why the decision was made not to perform DNA testing. It's likely that cost was a factor, but did anyone working on this case even have a doubt about the guilt of Bobby Jordan? Let's find out."

The two men divided the list of officers they could identify equally. John Cooksey was to contact the initial officer on the scene, Officer Lance Walker, as well as the two emergency medical technicians who had arrived at the same time. Jefferson Clay would talk to the three detectives who responded to the call. They would divide the crime scene technicians by each contacting and talking with two.

*****

Clay's first call was to his old acquaintance, Lieutenant Pete Kellner. When the call was put through by Kellner's secretary, the lieutenant was cordial.

"Jefferson, if the question is why we didn't do DNA testing in the Jordan murder case, the answer is pretty simple. The evidence all pointed to the husband as the suspect, DNA testing is expensive, and was even more expensive just a couple of years ago. In addition, not finding the husband's DNA on a sweater would not have proven anything. It really is that simple."

"But what if you had found DNA from a third person? Wouldn't that have been reason to question whether Bobby Jordan murdered his wife?" Clay asked.

"No, it probably wouldn't have. First, even today the database of known DNA samples which can be matched with newly collected evidence is very small. Most states don't routinely collect DNA from persons who are arrested. It's similar to the use of fingerprints in the 1920's. The national database was created, but there were not a lot of prints to match to for several years. There may come a time when DNA is as widely used as fingerprints, but it's not here yet." Kellner leaned back in his chair.

"Did you even consider or discuss the possibility of testing?" Clay persisted.

"I don't recall, but I doubt it. It was cutting edge science two years ago. Many of our investigators were only vaguely aware that it existed."

Pete Kellner's eyebrows furrowed as if he was trying to recall something. "You know, now that I think about it, a new kid who had just made detective may have asked about DNA testing in this case. It was T.J. Lawson and I think this was his first homicide. I gave him credit for even knowing what DNA was at the time. Why are you chasing this case, Jefferson? Am I missing something?"

Jefferson Clay liked Pete Kellner. He always left the impression of being an honest cop. "Pete, I began representing Bobby Jordan when he came to my office referred by his boss. After he was charged, I told him what a defense would cost and suggested that I might be able to get him a pretty good deal if he wanted to plead out.

Even though he had that young son who he was going to have to leave behind, he wouldn't consider pleading guilty. He said he couldn't because he didn't kill his wife. I believed him, but let him go to jail and get the court to appoint a lawyer to defend him. He got a good one in John Cooksey, but I have felt a little guilty about walking away from him because of the money. If I can prove he's innocent now, I'm going to do it."

The two men exchanged a few pleasantries about the Houston political climate and then ended the call. That afternoon Clay called one of the lead detectives on the case, Jimmy Starbuck. "Detective, this is Jefferson Clay. I am representing Bobby Jordan in an attempt to have some evidence tested for DNA. I would like to meet with you and discuss the case if you have time."

"Sorry Clay. I am not in the business of helping defense attorneys try to get convicts out of prison. I have no interest in discussing the case with you."

When Starbuck finished, Jefferson Clay tried an old tactic. "Are you that sure Jordan did the murder?"

"I'm absolutely sure he murdered his wife," Starbuck replied.

"Then why would you object to having DNA testing? If you're right, won't DNA testing just further prove your case? Did anyone suggest performing tests on the Houston Oilers sweater before charging Jordan?"

Jimmy Starbuck paused just long enough to make Jefferson Clay suspicious. "Why would we do that? Jordan was the murderer and we obviously had enough evidence to prove it. Look, I don't have time to argue with you." Starbuck placed his phone back on its cradle.

Clay's next call was to the Houston Homicide Division office. He asked for Detective Marcus Wilson and was advised that Wilson had retired. He asked for a phone number but was told by the secretary she would not provide contact information. The best he could do was convince her to contact the detective, give him Clay's office number and ask him to call. He held little hope he would ever hear from Wilson.

*****

Both Clay and Cooksey had thriving law practices, so each would spend time on the Jordan case sporadically. After Clay's first few dead-end attempts to talk to Starbuck and Wilson, he put the case on the back burner and concentrated on his paying clients. A month passed before the two lawyers met again to update each other on their progress.

Clay summarized his conversations with Lieutenant Kellner and his other two attempts to talk to detectives. He mentioned that the lieutenant had told him a young detective suggested DNA testing and that the suggestion had been ignored.

Cooksey had little to add except that the first officer on the scene, Lance Walker, believed Jordan was in shock when he first arrived at the home. While this was interesting, it had no impact on an argument to test the sweater.

John Cooksey also told Clay that one of the evidence technicians suggested to the detectives that the murder scene might be an appropriate opportunity for utilizing the fairly new science of gathering DNA samples. The technician advised Cooksey his idea was rejected at the scene, but this was not an unusual response at the time. DNA testing was very expensive and police departments across the nation generally didn't routinely engage in such testing.

He pointed out that over the few years since the Jordan murder case, investigators had accepted this new science and now gathering and testing such evidence was becoming a routine part of working any major crime scene. The evidence technician pointed out that if the same crime scene was recreated today, it would be as likely that DNA would be a major consideration in working the scene as it was unlikely when Regina Jordan was murdered.

Both men were discouraged with their progress at interviewing the officers, but both agreed to complete their follow-up by late February and prepare for the hearing to be held in March.

The next day, Jefferson Clay left the criminal court complex where he had taken care of an unrelated matter for another client. Since he was relatively close, he decided to go to the homicide office and try to catch Detective Lawson for a face-to-face conversation.

He asked the receptionist if Lawson was available. Within a few minutes Lawson stepped into the waiting room, introduced himself, and invited Clay to follow him to an interview room where they could talk.

"How can I help you?" Lawson began after they were seated.

"I am representing a client who was convicted of murdering his wife. My understanding is that you did some work on the case and I am attempting to interview all those who were involved in the investigation. My client is Bobby Jordan. Do you recall working on that case?"

Jefferson Clay sensed no hostility or wariness that defense attorneys often experience when discussing cases with law enforcement officers as he looked at T.J. Lawson.

"You never forget the first homicide you go out on and that was my first after I was promoted," the detective began, "but I'm afraid I can't help you much. I went to the scene with two other detectives on the morning of the murder and I did a little leg work over the next few days, but I caught another case and didn't do much more on the Jordan case. I'll be glad to answer any questions you might have, but I doubt that I can be much help." Lawson looked at Clay as if he was expecting another question.

"Detective, I am in the process of asking the trial court to authorize further testing on some of the evidence. There was a Houston Oilers sweater tagged as evidence in the case. When I talked to Lieutenant Kellner, he said you had suggested performing DNA tests on the sweater. Is that correct?"

"I did ask about DNA testing, but there was no interest in the idea. I was new to homicide and didn't push it," Lawson answered.

"Why did you suggest it?" Clay asked.

"Well, as I said, it was my first case and it seemed to me at the time that we came to a rather quick conclusion that the husband had killed her. I guess I was trying to slow things down a bit. Today it would pretty much be routine. But it was new science then.

What are you hoping to prove if you get the court to do the testing? You know the jury must have been pretty confident in the evidence. As I recall, the jury wasn't out too long before finding him guilty." Lawson seemed to be genuinely interested in the case.

"You know, detective, the defense usually isn't trying to *prove* anything. Bobby Jordan has always maintained that the Oilers sweater wasn't his. If it wasn't, why was it there and whose DNA might be found on it? We just think it's an avenue that should be explored. Do you recall anything else about the investigation? Do you have any notes?"

Lawson thought for a moment before answering. "I really don't recall anything that might help you, but all my notes are in the case file and I keep detailed notes. I don't think you are going to be able to get access to the case file, but my notes, as well as the other detectives' notes, should be there." The two men shook hands and Jefferson Clay left.

The morning following his conversation with Lawson, Clay received a call from the detective. "Mr. Clay. I thought about the Jordan case after you left yesterday and I remembered something you might want to know. I canvassed the neighborhood a day or two after the murder. One neighbor, who lives on a street behind the Jordan home, saw a car that she didn't recognize parked on the street during the same time frame as the murder. I'm not sure if there was any follow-up on the car because I was off the case pretty early as I said. It's not much, but I thought I would pass it on."

Clay thanked the detective and ended the call. T.J. Lawson leaned back in his chair and began thinking about the Jordan case. He wasn't being untruthful when he told Clay he didn't know if there was any follow-up on the mysterious car, but he knew Wilson wouldn't have taken on the job of checking it out on his own initiative. He also knew that Starbuck had been focused on making a case on Bobby Jordan and did not want to be sidetracked by issues that detracted from Jordan as the suspect.

Chapter Twenty Five

The motion to authorize DNA testing was heard on a Wednesday in March of 1994. Including the time he was in the Harris County jail, Bobby Jordan had been behind bars for four years. He did not attend the hearing because his presence wasn't needed. It could be handled by the attorneys.

Although disappointed that he was not there to hear the arguments made in court, Bobby, like most people who are not trained legal scholars, would have likely been bored by the arguments. His attorneys argued there had been dramatic advances not only in DNA science, but in the legal community's acceptance of such evidence since the Jordan trial. Because of these advances, the court should direct that the evidence be submitted for testing in an effort to ensure that justice be served.

The prosecution, on the other hand, argued that the defense counsel made no request at trial for such testing; and that simply referring to the failure of the prosecution to produce DNA testing during closing arguments, as John Cooksey had done, was not sufficient to now demand additional testing.

The judge did not issue a ruling on the motion immediately, but recessed until late in the afternoon, at which time court reconvened and the judge rendered a decision favoring the prosecution. Both Clay and

Cooksey were disappointed but not surprised. They agreed to meet back at Clay's office.

*****

When they were seated at a conference table in Clay's office, John Cooksey began speaking. "Jefferson, there's only one avenue I can see to go forward with the Jordan case. I think I should withdraw as co-counsel and you should file a new motion alleging ineffective counsel."

Jefferson Clay was not surprised. The idea had occurred to him also.

"Well, John, let's not be too hasty. I've been doing a little checking and there's a non-profit organization that has become very aggressive in working on cases such as this. It's called The Innocence Project. They are quite active in representing persons who have been convicted of crimes, but whose case files show legitimate possibility of a wrongful conviction.

"I think we should make contact with them and see if they might be interested in assisting in the Jordan case. If they have an interest, we'll get their opinion on the question of using the ineffective counsel argument.

"I also believe we should continue to interview those close to the case, especially those who testified, and see if we discover anything that might be helpful."

John Cooksey was relieved that Clay had not accepted his offer immediately. He knew alleging ineffective counsel might be their best opportunity to get Jordan's case back in the courtroom, but it was also personally devastating to him that the effectiveness of his skills as a criminal trial lawyer would be called into question as a result.

After more discussion, Clay volunteered to contact Regina Jordan's parents. John Cooksey would talk again to the car salesman. They then made an initial contact with The Innocence Project's office in New York City.

Pushing the speaker phone button, Clay dialed the phone and spoke briefly with the lady who answered the phone. When he explained that he and Cooksey were attorneys representing Bobby Jordan, she explained that she would forward a package to them to apply for assistance, but if he would hold for a moment, she would also connect him with one of the staff attorneys.

After a brief conversation regarding the case, the attorney assured the lawyers it was very likely they would be offered some assistance on the case of Bobby Jordan. They spoke briefly about a strategy, including the possibility of alleging Jordan did not receive adequate counsel from Cooksey, but the attorney advised them it would be necessary to review the case file before his office could recommend a strategy.

Jefferson Clay filed an appeal of the trial court's denial of the motion to perform DNA testing. Two weeks later, he was contacted by an attorney with The Innocence Project and they agreed to meet in mid-May to discuss the case in detail.

*****

Clay contacted Jenny White by phone. She agreed that she and her husband Robert would discuss the case with him at their home the following day. He arrived at two o'clock the next afternoon and introduced himself.

"I know that the death of your daughter has been a very difficult matter for both of you and I appreciate you agreeing to visit with me. As I advised Mrs. White when I called," Clay looked at Robert White as he continued talking, "I am representing your former son-in-law in an attempt to have DNA testing on some of the evidence that was gathered by police. There was a Houston Oilers sweater found at the scene. Bobby Jordan has always maintained it was not his. Do either of you recall whether he might have owned such a sweater?"

Robert White smiled slightly. "I doubt that he did. He was an avid Dallas Cowboys fan. I would have been surprised if he wore anything other than Cowboy clothing."

"Did you know about the sweater that was introduced as evidence?" Clay continued.

"I recall one of the detectives, probably Detective Starbuck, asking me if Bobby was an Oilers fan," Jenny White responded. "I told him I thought he was a fan of the Cowboys. That's all I remember."

"Was there anything that ever made you question whether Bobby was the one who murdered Regina?" Jefferson Clay knew he would have to be careful. If he offended either of the Whites he would be invited to leave.

Jenny White was the first to respond. "When we first learned our daughter was murdered, we didn't even consider that Bobby could have done this. But the more I talked to Detective Starbuck, the more obvious it became that he believed Bobby was the murderer. I began to believe he was guilty because I just saw how much the detective believed it. I don't think he would accuse someone of such a thing if he didn't know they did it.

"I did call a few days after Regina was killed and told one of the detectives about my conversation with B.J. when he stayed with us. But really nothing else made me doubt what the detective said."

Clay's pulse increased when he heard this. "I guess I don't recall seeing anything in the reports about your conversation with B.J. Can you tell me about that?"

"Yes. I was concerned about what B.J. might have seen and was worried that he might need to talk to someone about it. A two year old boy might not be mature enough to initiate such a conversation, so I asked him about the morning his mother was murdered. He told me a monster had hurt his mother. I asked him if the monster was his daddy and he said no, that his daddy had gone to work. That's really all there was to it. The detective didn't seem to think it was important."

"Which detective was it? Was it Detective Starbuck?" Jefferson Clay was taking notes now.

"No it wasn't him. I asked for him but they said he was out and told me I could talk to another detective who was working with him. I don't remember what his name was."

Jenny White stared down at the floor. It was obvious that talking about her daughter's death was causing her to become depressed. After a few questions for her husband, Jefferson Clay thanked them both and excused himself. He called John Cooksey as soon as he was back in his office.

*****

"John, do you recall anything in the file you received during discovery from the district attorney regarding a conversation Mrs. White had with one of the detectives. She called concerning Bobby's son B.J. telling her it was a monster, not his daddy, who hurt his mother?" Clay's voice betrayed his excitement.

"No, nothing I can remember, and I would remember that. Who told you about this?"

"I just left the White residence and she told me she had called and told the detectives about the conversation. If they had this information and didn't reveal it during discovery, we may be back in the game. I'll get back with you, but I want to get an affidavit from Mrs. White as soon as I can."

The two men ended the call. Jefferson Clay immediately called the White residence. After telling Jenny White the District Attorney had not revealed this information to the defense, he asked her to come to his office and give a signed statement. She agreed to do so the following morning after B.J. was off to school.

Chapter Twenty Six

When Jenny White arrived at Clay's office, her husband, Robert, was with her. Jefferson Clay sat with them at his conference table as Jenny wrote her statement on a yellow legal pad. Clay gave a similar pad to Robert White and asked him to write down his thoughts about whether Bobby Jordan might have owned or worn a Houston Oilers sweater.

After the Whites completed their statements, Clay's secretary quickly prepared them in printed documents. Each signed their statement and the secretary placed a notary seal next to their signatures.

*****

On May 17th of 1994, two attorneys, one from the New York office of The Innocence Project and the other from the Texas affiliate office in Dallas, met in Clay's office with Clay and Cooksey. After much discussion, it was agreed that John Cooksey would withdraw from the Jordan case and an appeal for a new trial would be filed alleging that his representation of Bobby Jordan at trial was not effective. As soon as the decision was made, John Cooksey shook the hand of each of the men, who he knew would be in a courtroom soon telling a judge that his legal skills were so severely lacking that Bobby deserved a new trial. Cooksey then left Clay's office.

In addition to that decision, the remaining three attorneys considered other issues that might warrant appealing the conviction of Bobby Jordan. Clay summarized the information that had been gathered up to that point.

First, he presented the Jenny White affidavit regarding her conversation with B.J. and the fact that she had told this to detectives prior to the trial and conviction of Bobby Jordan. The attorneys all agreed this information alone warranted an appeal for a new trial, but after Clay revealed his previous interview with Detective Lawson, they decided to ask the court to give the defense team access to the entire investigative file.

Lawson had told Clay that a neighbor who lived on the street behind the Jordan home saw a car that didn't belong in the neighborhood. It was parked on the street at the time the murder was believed to have occurred. Lawson also said he raised the issue of using DNA testing at the crime scene and one of the crime scene technicians also asked about such testing.

The attorneys agreed that before filing a motion for a new trial on the single issue, they would ask the court to grant them the right to review the entire investigative file. This would be based on what appeared to them to be the failure of the prosecutor's office to provide all the evidence before the trial took place. Their hope was they would discover additional evidence of inappropriate behavior by the prosecutor before filing a motion for a new trial.

And so began the long ordeal of waiting on court settings, presenting arguments and appealing decisions to higher courts. Bobby Jordan's lawyers would not get a final answer to their request to review the entire investigative file until November of 1997.

*****

Bobby had continued to adapt to life as a Texas convict. The most difficult thing for him to accept was the constant reminder that inmates were considered less than human by most of the prison staff. The interaction was cold, authoritarian and matter of fact. Rarely was there a question as simple as *How are things going?* Or *did you have a good day?*

He understood from talking to his cellmate that guards were trained not to allow personal relationships to develop with inmates. In fact, Matheson told him that at least two guards who worked in the license plate plant had been fired after being accused of that offense. One was caught bringing a magazine into the prison unit to give to an inmate. The other, a female guard, was simply accused of being too friendly with an inmate when she was observed on several occasions by a supervisor smiling when she spoke to him.

Relationships with inmates were no more relaxed than with the guards. No matter where he was, at work in the license plate plant, in the cafeteria or in the rec yard, there were always head games being played by inmates, gangs to watch for and avoid, and the ever present hostility that was as much a part of the atmosphere as the very air he breathed. The only place Bobby allowed the tenseness to leave his body was in his cell with his cellmate, Delbert Matheson. The two had not become friends; true to his word, Matheson just wanted to do his time and be left alone.

Infrequently, the two men engaged in conversation, but rarely did they talk about personal matters.

Bobby appreciated the respect he was shown by Mr. Martin, the supervisor whom he worked for since coming to the Wynne Unit. He was not friendly, but he was respectful. He was working at the license plate plant for nearly four years when Officer F. Fleming, a female guard, was assigned to the plant. She assisted each morning in conducting the count before allowing the inmates to begin work. Officer Fleming, like Mr. Martin, exhibited a degree of respect for inmates that most of the guards avoided. She never smiled and she never engaged in conversation except for business, but she did occasionally say *thank you* or *excuse me* when appropriate.

Fleming was a woman who knew her job. She was not unattractive, but she did not wear make-up on the job, nor did she have her uniforms tailored as some of the female guards did, a practice which always drew the attention of inmates. She was a single mother who appreciated having a job that paid more than secretarial work and she didn't intend to jeopardize it by making a mistake. She had been a corrections officer for over ten years, but never became jaded in her view of inmates. She knew that there, but by the grace of God, was one of her sons or brothers. She tried to treat everyone with respect and it didn't go unnoticed by Bobby Jordan.

The most devastating news Bobby had received since coming to the Wynne Unit occurred during a visit by his former father-in-law in late 1995 on a Saturday morning. Robert White told Bobby he and his wife would no longer be bringing B.J. to visit. White said that for the last several months, B.J. had cried and asked not to be taken to prison. He and his wife had decided it served no good purpose to require B.J. to make the visits. Knowing he had no control over the Whites' decision, Bobby offered no argument.

This single occurrence caused Bobby to seek some relief for the inner upheaval he was experiencing in his life. Even though he knew the lawyers were working to free him, so were lawyers for hundreds of other inmates in Texas and the chances of success were miniscule.

One day he took his cellmate Matheson up on the long standing offer to borrow a magazine. By sheer happenstance, the magazine contained an article about meditation. Fascinated by the article, he asked his sister and brother to send magazines and books regarding the subject. One book he received was a study of Zen Buddhism and he read it with fascination. Over time, he learned to relieve his mental anguish by practicing his own version of meditation and Zen-like behavior, but he never associated with any of the numerous religious groups that existed within the prison system.

*****

The various legal appeals wound their way through the slow judicial process. John Cooksey's initial procedural appeals were rejected as had been anticipated. The first appeal that had been filed on the court's denial to allow DNA testing was eventually sent back down from the appellate court to the trial court on a procedural error. The trial court quickly corrected the error and found for the prosecution once again. This second decision was again appealed by the Jordan defense team and the case lay in limbo for months awaiting the court's decision to schedule arguments by the attorneys.

The appeal regarding ineffective counsel was determined to be without merit at the trial court and the defense attorneys pushed this issue into the appellate court arena also. The defense motion to permit the defense attorneys to have access to the entire investigative file was granted by the trial court. The prosecutor's office promptly appealed that decision.

By January of 1997, the status of the three appeals was as follows: The appeal of the trial court's decision not to require DNA testing had been heard and the appellate court ruled against the defense. The appeal by the prosecutor of the trial court's decision to permit the defense access to the entire investigative file had also been denied, allowing Bobby Jordan some small hope. The appeal of ineffective counsel by the defense was denied. All three cases were appealed to the Texas Court of Criminal Appeals, the court that would make the final decisions and the rough equivalent of the Texas Supreme Court which hears non-criminal appeals. The defense pursued the right to conduct DNA testing, as well as a new trial, based on ineffective counsel. The prosecution appealed the decision to allow the defense access to their files.

*****

As summer approached, Assistant District Attorney James Southard, who was assigned to handle the appeals in the Jordan murder case, dropped by the office of Assistant D.A. Johnny Remington. Remington sat through the entire trial, selected the jurors, questioned some of the witnesses, and assisted the two more seasoned attorneys, Paul Scarsdale, who was now the district attorney, and Bradley Vance Thompson, who now sat on the Texas Court of Criminal Appeals.

After explaining his role in the Jordan appeals, Southard began. "Johnny, there are three issues on this Jordan case. I'm pretty comfortable in arguing against this belated attempt to do DNA testing. I am also confident in arguing that John Cooksey provided an adequate defense of Jordan. But I need some help with the information that was withheld from discovery before trial. Can you help me with that?"

Remington was thoughtful in his response. "You know, I was as green as could be when I assisted with that case. I remember it well because when I reviewed the file before trial, I was convinced we couldn't get a conviction on circumstantial evidence, and that was all we had.

I wasn't involved in preparing the files for discovery and didn't review what was given to the defense. But I was surprised that the only document regarding what the little boy told his grandmother about the murder was just a handwritten note in the detective's file. I thought Cooksey made a huge error when he didn't raise that issue and perhaps even put the kid on the witness stand; but I guess I judged him too quickly. Apparently our office didn't give him that information during discovery."

"Do you think it should have been given to the defense?" Southard asked.

"You know, one thing I still hang on to from my law school days is that a prosecutor's job is to seek justice. It's easy to lose sight of that when you walk into this office every day knowing that one of the primary indicators of the value of a prosecutor's work is his conviction rate. But I still believe we shouldn't bend the rules and if we make an honest mistake we should admit it and try to correct it if possible. I would have erred on the side of the defense on this one. I would have probably agreed to the DNA testing when Clay and Cooksey appealed that one too," Johnny Remington responded bluntly.

"My job is to defend the decisions that were made at the time, but your assessment doesn't offer much encouragement for that position. I guess I need to talk to the boss and see if he remembers why they didn't produce the handwritten note," Southard said as he rose from his chair.

James Southard left Remington and walked directly to District Attorney Paul Scarsdale's office. He asked the receptionist if she might squeeze him in between appointments to see the boss. Within a few minutes, Scarsdale's personal secretary walked into the reception area to advise Southard the District Attorney had ten minutes before his next appointment and would see him. He followed her into Scarsdale's office.

"Come in, James. How are you doing? Have a seat," Scarsdale greeted Southard.

"Hi, boss. I'll get right to the point. I know you're pressed for time. I was assigned to handle the appeals on the Jordan murder case. One of the appeals alleges that we didn't turn over some important information during discovery and they want access to the entire file. Specifically, they alleged we didn't give them information we had about a conversation the guy's kid had with the mother-in-law. It had to do with the kid saying his dad was at work when a monster hurt his mom.

"But when I reviewed the file, I also found that we didn't give them some information about a car that was spotted behind the murder scene on the morning of the murder. The defense team must not be aware of that. I checked and we didn't include it in discovery either.

"Can you remember who put together the packet for discovery and why we didn't include those items?"

James Southard was not intimidated by asking the boss these questions. He assumed Scarsdale would expect him to thoroughly review the case.

"You know I handled most of that case. Thompson sat in and made sure he got all the press, but I did most of the work. I put together the discovery and Thompson approved it.

"Regarding both those items, our position was that they were nothing more than non-essential information obtained by the detectives. As you know, many things we learn during an investigation are not revealed in discovery for a variety of reasons, but in this case it was simply that it had no bearing on the case." Scarsdale looked at his watch and then returned his gaze to Southard.

"Well, boss, looking at it in hindsight, I think it's going to be a gamble as to whether the appellate judges will agree with you. The appeal is a little unusual. They are using this one item as an argument to get access to the entire investigative file. Of course, if they are successful, they'll have the information on the car in the neighborhood too. Then they'll ask for a new trial." Southard stood as if to leave.

"James, you know we have to fight this thing as vigorously as we can. We don't need to retry a murder case. I'm sure you will have a convincing argument for the court."

Southard held out his hand. "Boss, you know I'll do my best. I'm just letting you know this one isn't going to be that simple."

As Southard walked out of the office, he thought Remington might be onto something. For the district attorney to claim the information was withheld because it was not essential to the case was surprising. It might not be essential to the prosecution, but it very well could have blown the case wide-open for the defense, especially since the entire case was built on circumstantial evidence.

Chapter Twenty Seven

The first appeal was heard by the Texas Court of Criminal Appeals in late summer. By November, Jefferson Clay received the news that the court held that the defense team would be permitted to review the investigative file. He called the district attorney immediately, but didn't receive a return call until four days later.

On a Friday afternoon the week before Thanksgiving, James Southard made the call to Clay. "Mr. Clay. Congratulations! You did a good job arguing the case. The Justices saw it your way."

Jefferson Clay wasted no time getting to the point. "Thank you and thanks for returning my call. When can we schedule a review of the case file?"

"Well, one of the things I wanted to discuss with you was whether we might be able to come to an agreement to short circuit this entire process. Our team met with the boss yesterday; he has authorized me to make you an offer.

"We think everyone will be well served if we can accommodate your client's desire to be released from prison while at the same time dismissing the appeals and potential retrial of the murder case. So what we are willing to offer you is, to ask the court to set aside the conviction, have your client plead guilty to negligent homicide and we will recommend a sentence of time served."

Clay was silent for a moment. This offer was a surprise. "There must be some really damaging details in the case file! I'm surprised, after all the media interviews by both this district attorney and the previous one, during which they were adamant my client should never be released to prey upon society, that Scarsdale has changed his mind."

"Look, Clay. It's just a practicality and it's an opportunity for your client to get out of prison. I'd think long and hard about the offer before rejecting it. There's nothing earth shattering in the file and your other appeals may be denied."

"Oh, I will take the offer to my client, but you need to know that he chose to go to prison rather than plead guilty to a murder he has always said he didn't commit. It may be that all these years in prison have caused him to rethink that, but I'm betting it hasn't. I'll go to Huntsville next week. I'll let you know."

*****

The following Monday, Jefferson Clay had a case set to be heard in District Court. He made the appearance. When finished in court, he called his co-counsels with The Innocence Project. He told them of the offer. The staff attorney who lived in Texas, Jack Whittington, agreed immediately to meet him at the Wynne Prison Unit two days later to advise their client. Clay then arranged the visit with Bobby Jordan at eleven a.m. on Wednesday.

Whittington and Clay met in the visitor parking lot and entered the prison together. After submitting to the procedure for attorney visits with inmates, they were escorted to a room where Bobby Jordan sat waiting at a grey metal table.

"How are you doing, Bobby?" Clay asked.

"I'm still here. Do you ever think of how ridiculous that question is, Mr. Clay? In prison for seven years; lost my wife and my son; no more of life's dreams. I'll let you try to figure out the answer." Bobby was not in a good mood.

"Well, we've got some good news for you. The Texas Court of Criminal Appeals ruled late last week that we can have access to the entire investigative file on your wife's murder. In addition, the district attorney has made a proposal that could get you out of here within a couple of weeks."

Jefferson Clay stopped and looked for a reaction on Bobby's face. He saw none and that troubled him. He guessed his client had sunk into a deep depression.

"District attorney says he will agree to set aside your conviction and allow you to plead guilty to a lesser charge for time already served. Of course, it is just a recommendation to the judge, but very likely to be accepted. We probably need to make a decision quickly because the Court will be rendering decisions in the other appeals any day now and I don't know how that might affect the offer."

"So, I've spent seven years in prison and lost everything for the same deal you tried to get me to take before the trial?" Sarcasm dripped from his words.

Jack Whittington, who had been introduced to Bobby for the first time a few minutes earlier, decided to speak. "Mr. Jordan, we're with you all the way regardless of whether you decide to take this deal or not. It is an important offer for a couple of reasons.

First, it allows you to be in control of your destiny for the first time in seven years. You get to make the decision whether you walk out of here a free man.

"The second reason is the very fact that the district attorney made the offer gives us insight into what they think our chances are moving forward. Now they will tell us, already did tell Mr. Clay, that they're making the offer to save the government the cost of continuing to fight. But they have also probably assessed the possibility that we could win a new trial and testing of the now infamous Houston Oilers sweater for DNA. So, it's good news, no matter what you decide."

Bobby sat looking down at the table for nearly a minute before he looked back at the two attorneys and spoke. "I don't know what the rules are about offers from the district attorney, but here's my deal for him. He agrees to test the sweater and if my DNA is found on it I'll drop all appeals and make the last little mental adjustment to accept that I am a convict and won't ever be anything else. If only my wife's DNA is on it, we move forward with the appeals. But if someone else's DNA is found on the sweater, he clears my name and releases me.

"If he doesn't like that deal, screw him! I don't have anything to look forward to in here, but I don't see much of a life out there either. Everything I ever had or wanted has been taken away. I have to concentrate on thinking positive every night to keep my sanity. I told you seven years ago I wouldn't plead guilty because I didn't kill my wife. That hasn't changed."

Bobby suddenly relaxed as he sat at the table. Jefferson Clay thought he saw the beginning of a slight smile appear on Bobby's lips. Clay thought how good it must feel to this man whose life had been dictated by others for so long to finally get to make a decision about his life.

"We'll relay your offer to him. I'm not optimistic about his response," Clay said.

"Wait a minute." Jack Whittington moved forward in the grey metal chair on which he was seated. "Do you mind if we try to get some news coverage of your case and what you just said about your offer?"

"What could it hurt?" Bobby responded immediately, "It's not like I have to worry about my great reputation in the community."

Jefferson Clay interrupted. "Well, Bobby, why don't you leave that decision to your legal team? Jack and I will discuss a public event with the media as a strategy. We'll get back with you after we get an answer from the district attorney."

The lawyers rose and exited the interview room. When they were outside the prison gates walking toward their cars, Clay stopped, looking at Whittington.

"I don't want you to misconstrue what I am about to say. Before we take Bobby's offer or anything else to the news media, I want to make sure we do it as an end game for his case; not for a publicity stunt to get news coverage for any other reason."

"I understand your concern, Jefferson. I think we run the offer by the district attorney first, but if he rejects it, I believe we are obligated to consider creating some outside pressure.

"I assure you that if we do, my only intent is to help our client. If you think it's about promoting The Innocence Project, you're dead wrong. Look at our history and don't insult me with innuendo. Why don't you visit with the district attorney, let me know what he says, and if he doesn't have a good response, we'll meet next week to discuss this in more detail." Whittington held out his hand.

As the two men shook hands Jefferson Clay responded, "I was out of line. The Innocence Project is the best thing that has happened to the criminal justice system in the U.S. in a life time. Forgive me."

Chapter Twenty Eight

Clay called Assistant District Attorney James Southard when he returned to his office from Huntsville. "Mr. Southard, I've just returned from visiting my client, Bobby Jordan. I discussed your offer with him and I have a counter.

"We want agreement from your office to test the sweater. If my client's DNA is found on the sweater we'll ask the court to dismiss all our pending appeals and it's over. If no DNA is discovered or if only Regina Jordan's DNA is on it, we move forward with the appeals and there is no deal; but if DNA not identified as my client's or Regina's is found on the sweater, your office joins us in clearing Bobby's name with the court and having him released."

James Southard was quick to respond. "Well, I'll bet you would like that deal. If your client loses he's no worse off than he is right now. If it's a draw he still has a shot at the appeals and in your third scenario he wins outright without any real proof or significant indication that a third party actually committed the murder.

"I'm afraid we can't consider your proposal seriously. We were hesitant to make the offer we did because of the violent nature of the murder. I suppose we'll just have to move forward in the courts."

Clay was not impressed with the response. "You know, James, I don't believe you and I have ever worked together on a case, but I've worked with a number of your co-workers and with your boss, Scarsdale, in the past. One thing I believe all of them will tell you is that I am not into puffery or idle threats to the opposing counsel. I believe in dealing with facts.

"With that said, I am telling you unequivocally that I am convinced my client is not a murderer and I intend to continue to pursue this case more vigorously than anything I have ever worked on. If you guys are wrong, this is going to be the most embarrassing situation Scarsdale has had during his term in office. He wasn't the elected representative when evidence was withheld from the defense, but he is calling the shots now, while keeping an innocent man in prison. So, with that said, tell me when I can meet with you to receive the file on the investigation."

"It will be ready for you on Friday." Southard's response was curt.

That exchange ended the phone conversation and Clay immediately called Jack Whittington. "Jack, they rejected the offer. No surprise there, but I've been thinking about your idea of involving the media. I pick up the file on Friday. If you can drive in on Monday, I suggest we spend a couple of hours reviewing it and then see if we can peddle a story to the Chronicle.

"I don't want to hold a media event, but if a credible reporter does a story about Bobby's case, and if we go after him for stalling the release of an innocent man, the district attorney may reconsider his position."

Jack Whittington agreed to drive to Houston Sunday evening. The two men would meet Monday morning.

Chapter Twenty Nine

On Friday morning Clay arrived at the district attorney's office and advised the receptionist he was there to pick up a file. After a short phone conversation, she advised Clay that Mr. Southard would be right out. A few minutes passed before James Southard walked through the door and greeted Clay.

"Good morning Mr. Clay. If you'll follow me, we have a copy of the file ready for you." Southard was obviously not happy as he turned and walked to a small office next to the reception desk. As the two men entered the office, Southard pointed to a corner where Clay saw four cardboard boxes with his name written on the end of each with a grease pencil.

"There you are. Our receptionist, Ms. Smith, may be able to find a two wheel dolly for you if you didn't bring one." With that, Southard turned and walked back through the door into the bowels of the district attorney's office suite.

Rather than ask for assistance, Clay carried the boxes, two at a time, to his car. He then drove to his office and repeated the task, taking the boxes to a conference room. When finished, he realized how badly he needed a more rigorous exercise routine.

He left his office early that afternoon. He knew he would be spending most of the weekend sorting and reading the case file. This afternoon and evening he would spend with his wife of thirty years, who, though tolerant of his irregular and sometimes long work schedule, expected that he carve time from that schedule for quality time with her. He would take her to a nice restaurant this evening and be back at the office by ten on Saturday morning.

*****

Clay was in his office by nine-thirty the next morning and began by spreading the files from the first box across the conference table. He soon realized he had already reviewed every item from this box. It included the police reports, a copy of the indictment, arrest records, and statements of Bobby Jordan and a number of witnesses. All these documents had been provided before the trial to either he or John Cooksey. The second box contained copies of the court documents pertaining to the various appeals that had been filed in the case. Clay soon realized there was nothing new in this box either.

The third box of material contained court documents regarding Clay's withdrawal from the case, the appointment of John Cooksey as counsel, as well as a few notes about various jurors presumably jotted down while the jury was being picked. Although it was interesting to read the observations of the prosecutors regarding potential jurors, there was nothing that was not routine.

It took Clay nearly three hours to review the files from the first three boxes. He decided to walk down the street to a local deli and order a sub sandwich to take back to his office for lunch. After returning with the sandwich and a large paper cup of sweet tea, he lifted the final box onto the table and laid its contents into two separate stacks of paper. While eating, he pulled a paper from the top of the stack and saw a pink memo slip that had been torn from a message pad similar to those used in most offices, including his own.

The note had Starbuck written at the top. Clay read the message. *'Mrs. White called. Said her grandson told her his daddy (Jordan) was at work when a monster hurt his mom. I told her I would pass the info on to you since you are who she asked for. Let me know if you have questions.'* The note was signed M.W.

So this was the information that had been withheld. Clay hoped he would discover more as he dug through the files. He placed the note on a corner of the table and continued reviewing the stack of papers.

After having looked over more than half of the first stack and finding nothing more, he saw a page from a yellow legal pad covered with very neatly written block print notes. The bottom of the page had T.J.L. written on it. Clay assumed this was Lawson's notes. He looked over the page and found a couple of interesting entries.

First was the reference Lawson had made to him about a suspicious car. Lawson noted the name and address of the woman who told him about the car being on the street as well as her rather vague description of the car. She called it a little foreign car that was burgundy colored. She was sure it did not belong in the neighborhood.

The second entry that piqued his curiosity was a note Lawson had made asking (presumably to himself) *'Why no DNA testing? Why is the lieutenant rushing to file charges? Why not check the car salesman's statement that Regina brought her mother with her to get her car serviced because her husband was suspicious?* Just after that question was a final thought. *Why am I questioning a room full of experienced homicide investigators?*

Jefferson Clay was not sure the prosecutor had an obligation to reveal to the defense a detective's misgivings about the way the case was developed; but he was positive that the information about the suspicious car should have been divulged.

He finished his sandwich and tea before delving into the second stack of files from the last box. Halfway through the papers he found no additional information he believed was helpful. Then he picked up the next item in the stack which was a manila file folder with 'Regina Jordan' hand written on the tab. As he began to look through the contents of the file, he realized it contained Detective Starbuck's notes and other information the detective had gathered during the investigation.

As he shuffled through the pages, a message note fell to the table. It was addressed to Starbuck just as the other message from M.W. was, but this note was written in a professional and much neater handwriting. Clay was sure it was a woman's handwriting; probably a message taken by the secretary.

In the subject line were written the words 'Jordan case/suspicious car' and the body of the note contained only the name Horace Baldwin and a local phone number. Clay quickly reached for the notes from Lawson and confirmed that the witness Lawson had referred to was not named Baldwin. He then studied the note for several minutes before picking up the phone and calling the number.

After two rings the phone was answered by a man's voice. "Hello."

"Mr. Baldwin?"

"Yes, this is Horace Baldwin."

"Mr. Baldwin, my name is Jefferson Clay. I am an attorney and I am working on a murder case that occurred several years ago. The victim's name was Regina Jordan."

Baldwin interrupted with a sarcastic tone. "You mean after all these years someone is interested in hearing about the car I saw behind the Jordan home that morning? Don't you think it's a little late for that?"

Jefferson Clay physically felt his pulse increase as he heard the words. "I'm interested Mr. Baldwin. Do you live on the street behind the Jordan residence?"

"I live directly behind and on the same side of the street as that home. There is a vacant lot behind that home and my house faces the vacant lot. My address is 223 Braxton. Same house numbers as the Jordan home."

"Mr. Baldwin, can I meet you at your home to discuss this with you? I am representing Mr. Jordan who was convicted of killing his wife and we just learned that you might have information about the murder."

"Come on! I'll be here all afternoon."

Chapter Thirty

After ending the call, Jefferson Clay quickly straightened the items on the conference table, making sure he kept the small stack of papers he had not yet looked at separate from the other files. He then left the office to meet with Horace Baldwin.

Although he had known Bobby Jordan's address since the first time they met, Clay had never actually been on the street. Because he was driving into the neighborhood, he decided to drive by the home before meeting with Baldwin. As he passed the house he saw a young father in the front yard playing with his son, who appeared to be about five years old. The home held secrets of the Jordan family that this new owner was oblivious to. Clay drove on and was soon at the home of Horace Baldwin.

Before he could ring the doorbell, the door opened and Baldwin invited him inside. After handshakes and introductions, the two men were seated on overstuffed matching chairs in a room that was furnished as a formal living room.

"Mr. Baldwin, since I learned that you had some information regarding the murder only this morning, maybe it would be best if you just told me whatever you told the police at the time." Clay sat back in his chair.

"I never told the police anything. I called the main police department number and told the operator I might have some information regarding the murder. This would have been the day after it happened, because I didn't even know what had happened over there until I read the newspaper the next morning.

"At any rate, the operator transferred my call and the woman who answered said it was the homicide office. I told her I lived behind the house where the murder happened and I saw a suspicious car that morning parked in front of the vacant lot behind the house. She told me the detectives were all out of the office and she would give them my message. The next time I heard from anyone about it was when you called earlier today." As Baldwin spoke he seemed irritated that his call had been ignored.

"Well, can I ask what you saw?" Jefferson Clay had interviewed hundreds of witnesses and knew it was often necessary to pull the information needed from them.

"Yes. I go out every morning at a few minutes before seven and let my dog run around the front yard for about thirty minutes or so. When I went out that morning, I saw the car parked across the street.

"I remembered the car because a guy driving it had knocked on my door about a week earlier and wanted to paint my house. I didn't hire him, but I remembered the car. It was a dark red colored Toyota. The little one, I think it's called a Corolla."

Clay interrupted, "Did you get the license number?"

"Actually I did. I kept it for a long time but I must have thrown it away because after you called I looked for it in my desk and couldn't find it. I'll look again if you think it would help."

"I would really appreciate that," Clay responded. "Can you tell me what the guy looked like?"

"Yeah, he was about thirty, kinda thin and spindly. Didn't look too clean, dirty jeans and a tee shirt. He looked like a druggy to me. Long dirty hair, pale complexion like he never got out much in the sun, circles under his eyes and bad teeth. Just the kinda guy you wouldn't want hangin' around your home. I went back in the house and when I looked back outside about an hour later the car was gone."

"Did you call the detectives back when no one contacted you?"

Horace Baldwin frowned. "No! I don't think it's my responsibility to make sure they do their job. I figured they must have already known about the car and didn't need my help. Then, a week or so later, I read in the paper that the husband did it, so I decided what I saw wasn't important. I still think they should have had the courtesy of calling me though."

"Are you willing to come to my office on Monday and give me an affidavit about what you saw and the fact that no one at the police department ever followed up with you?"

"I'll be glad to. I wanted to help or I wouldn't have called. Do you think this guy might have been involved?"

"Mr. Baldwin, I don't have a clue, but I know my client Mr. Jordan didn't kill his wife and the police should have followed up on your information. If they had followed up, Mr. Jordan might not have spent the last several years in prison."

After agreeing that Baldwin would be at Clay's office at ten Monday morning, Clay left the Baldwin home and returned to his work with the files. He sat at the conference table at four-thirty and continued to examine the files until nearly six, but he found no additional bombshells.

When he was sure he had thoroughly reviewed the file, he sat back in his chair. Jack Whittington had given Clay his home phone number. He decided to call and tell him what he'd discovered. Upon dialing the number it was answered by a female.

"Is Jack in? This is Jefferson Clay in Houston."

"Yes, Mr. Clay. One moment please." Clay waited for nearly two minutes before Whittington picked up the phone.

"Sorry I took so long, Jefferson. My wife has me in the back yard moving plants around and digging up bushes. What's going on?"

Jefferson Clay was a little embarrassed at having interrupted Whittington's weekend with the news. It wasn't as if they were young attorneys with bright-eyed enthusiasm.

"I'm sorry, Jack. I probably shouldn't have called, but I picked up the files from the district attorney yesterday and I've spent all day reading them.

I found something I think is going to be a big help. There is a second witness who saw the suspicious car and although he called the police to tell them, they never called him back. I found the message in a file and called the number. Luckily he still has the same phone number and was willing to talk. He'll be at my office at ten Monday to give us an affidavit. I guess I just wanted to tell someone about the good luck."

"That's great Jefferson. Sounds like we'll have a busy day Monday; and by the way, don't ever hesitate to call me with good news. It is a rare commodity in this business and we should savor the moment."

The two men said their goodbyes and Clay left his office. He decided not to work on Sunday. He would start fresh Monday morning with Jack Whittington at his side.

Chapter Thirty One

On Monday, prior to Horace Baldwin's arrival at the office, the two lawyers reviewed briefly the information Clay had gleaned from the files. As they were finishing the review, Clay's secretary advised that Mr. Baldwin had arrived. Clay prepared the written statement for Baldwin, who read and signed it. He left the office in less than an hour.

Once Baldwin was gone, Jack Whittington began the same task Clay had performed on Saturday; going through each box of files as if he was the first to have the opportunity. Jefferson Clay called a reporter with the Houston Chronicle whom he had given several previous interviews to regarding cases in which he was involved. They agreed to meet at Clay's office at three that afternoon.

After a short lunch break during which Whittington told Clay he had found nothing new in the files, the two men discussed their pending conversation with the reporter. It was agreed that Clay would take the lead since he knew the reporter, but both agreed that Whittington's association with The Innocence Project meant the reporter was likely to have an interest in the organization's involvement. The reporter arrived a few minutes before three and the attorneys met with him in the conference room where the files lay in several stacks on the table.

The story, at least the story that Jefferson Clay wanted to see, was one of the district attorney concealing important information that, if given to the jury, would have resulted in Bobby Jordan never having gone to prison. If he sensed the reporter was buying into that theory, he would stress the importance of getting Bobby out of prison and the obstinate position that District Attorney Scarsdale was taking to block all attempts to find the truth. In addition, he hoped the reporter would emphasize in print that there was likely a violent murderer on Houston's streets still stalking victims in the area.

When asked by the reporter, Clay stopped short of saying that the district attorney's office had engaged in willfully concealing evidence. He did, however, suggest that was a question the office should have to answer, since they had known about two separate witnesses who saw a suspicious car parked behind the victim's home that morning. In addition, the fact that the victim's son had said that Bobby Jordan was at work when the murder occurred was known to them. Neither of these facts had been revealed to the defense prior to Clay's having obtained a court order to see the prosecutor's file.

After more than two hours of discussion, the reporter thanked the two attorneys, told them the story would likely appear in print late in the week or early next week. He told them he wanted to interview some of the people involved in the prosecution, including the former and current district attorneys. In addition, he intended to talk with Jenny White and the new witness, Horace Baldwin.

Clay usually read the morning newspaper with his first cup of coffee before leaving home for the office; but beginning the following Thursday, his routine changed. Even before pouring a cup of coffee, he would retrieve the Chronicle from the front yard and check for the story. It didn't appear in the newspaper until the following Tuesday.

Front page headlines read "**Lawyers accuse District Attorney of withholding evidence and hampering release of innocent man in murder case**". Delighted with the headline, although he did think it was a little 'over-the-top', he eagerly read the entire story. It was just what he wanted.

He might have been even more delighted had he known that the revelation of a witness named Horace Baldwin had the entire District Attorney's office scrambling. As soon as D.A. Paul Scarsdale read the story over breakfast that morning he called Johnny Remington at his home and caught him just as he was leaving for the office.

"Johnny, who the hell is this guy Horace Baldwin? The Chronicle is identifying him as a witness in the Jordan murder case. I've never heard of him before."

"I have no idea what you are talking about," Remington responded.

"Haven't you read the paper this morning?" Scarsdale asked. "My God, they're crucifying us for hiding witnesses and plotting to keep an innocent man in prison. Get the newspaper and meet me at the office as soon as you can get there. Find out where Southard is this morning. He's quoted in the article as saying our office won't have any comment because the appeals are still pending. Get his ass in my office as well."

After ending the phone call, both men rushed to leave their homes and drive to the office. Johnny

Remington grabbed the morning paper and began reading as he jogged to his car. By the time he arrived at the office he had finished the story and barely avoided two collisions while driving with the newspaper held over the steering wheel.

In Paul Scarsdale's office, the three men sat around a small conference table. Each had a copy of the morning's Houston Chronicle. Paul Scarsdale began speaking. "James, why didn't you tell me this was coming?"

James Southard looked directly at his boss. "I did! I told you I talked to this guy and he was doing a story on the appeal of Jordan's murder conviction."

Scarsdale's voice grew more intense. His anger at Southard was unmistakable. "I don't mean that there was going to be a story! I mean about this witness. Why didn't you tell all of us?"

"Because I didn't know about it!" Southard raised his voice to meet that of his boss. He was a confident lawyer and employee. He wouldn't be bullied. "The reporter called and wanted to talk about the case. As I told you just after talking to him, I told him the case is still pending and we wouldn't have a comment. That was the extent of the conversation and I believe, if you will read the story, that's what he printed!" The sarcasm in Southard's tone did not go unnoticed by the district attorney, but he let it go.

"Alright, does anyone know who this witness is? Johnny, do you remember him?" The D.A.'s voice was lower.

Remington had barely arrived at the office when he began to look through the Jordan file. But moments into the task, he was summoned to the boss's office.

"Boss, I have never heard the name. I started going through the file when your secretary called me for this meeting."

"Well, get back to it. As soon as either of you know what this is about get back in here. I'll just be unavailable if any of the other news outlets call until we have a handle on it." Scarsdale rose from his chair.

Remington and Southard also stood and exited Scarsdale's office. In the hallway, they agreed to work together looking through the files. It was two hours before Southard picked up the phone message that had led Jefferson Clay to Horace Baldwin.

The lawyers knew that Baldwin had never actually talked to the police or their office because of what was reported in the newspaper article. They decided that before calling him, they would try to determine why he had not been contacted. The place to start was by talking to the person the message was directed to.

Remington picked up the phone, called Lieutenant Kellner and asked him if he could have Detective Starbuck at a meeting with the district attorney's team assigned to the Jordan case. Remington had been around long enough to know not to burn Starbuck with his boss before finding out what had happened. If a detective thought you were going over his head he was unlikely to be very cooperative and would be more difficult to work with in the future.

The meeting took place in Remington's office at two o'clock that afternoon. Scarsdale was bouncing off the walls for information, but Remington ignored the outbursts each time his boss called. Remington simply told him that as soon as they had the information he would be the first to get it.

When Starbuck, Southard and Remington had greeted each other and taken seats in a small conference room, Remington handed the message to Starbuck.

"Detective, I'm sure you've read the morning paper. This message, addressed to you, is the only reference we've found in the file regarding Horace Baldwin. Can you tell us anything about him or why we didn't know about him?"

"Yeah, I can tell you something about it." Starbuck's tone was both arrogant and defensive. "I got this message a couple of days after he called. I was busy running down other information on the case, so it was a couple of weeks before I looked at it again. We had already made the case on Jordan and he'd been charged with the murder.

"That morning I was on my way over here to meet with the district attorney and his investigator; that's the former D.A., Judge Thompson, to do a wrap-up on the case before closing our end of it. I brought the message with me, told Thompson and the investigator about it, and gave it to them. End of story."

"Did you tell them you had not called the guy?" Southard asked.

Starbuck's irritation was clear in his voice as he answered. "Well, what do you think counselor? Certainly I told them. What are you guys trying to do, find a scapegoat for the bad press?"

"Why didn't you talk to Baldwin?" Remington's question was direct and without emotion.

"I was busy with other things. By the time I remembered the message the case was in the hands of your office. I assumed if you guys thought it was important, you would follow up with the guy."

"Do you remember who the investigator was at the meeting with you and Judge Thompson?" Remington asked.

"Sure do. It was Nelson Bartosh. I attended his funeral two weeks ago. He died six weeks after he retired." Starbuck stared out the window as if thinking about the funeral.

Chapter Thirty Two

Johnny Remington and James Southard walked out of the office with Detective Starbuck. As he pushed the button for an elevator, the two lawyers entered District Attorney Paul Scarsdale's office. They briefed him on having found the message in the file and their conversation with Starbuck.

"Ok, so did you talk to Thompson? Does he remember the conversation about Baldwin?"

"We haven't talked to him yet, but I'll try to catch him before he leaves his office this afternoon," Remington replied.

"Well, regardless of what he remembers, we've got egg on our face. Get someone out to take a statement from this witness and see if there is anything to follow up on. In the morning I want to meet again and look over our entire strategy on this thing. I can't believe it is becoming so unmanageable."

Remington left the meeting and walked across the street to the criminal courts building. Although Judge Thompson was no longer a Harris County judge, he still maintained an office in the building. If the court was not scheduled to hear cases, usually in the state's capital city of Austin, he could be found here.

Johnny Remington went directly to Judge Thompson's office behind several courtrooms on the fourth floor. After checking with the judge, his secretary escorted Remington to his office.

He explained the details of what had been learned since the article appeared in the newspaper earlier that morning. He then asked the judge what his recollection of the meeting with Starbuck was.

"I'm sure I met with Starbuck, probably several times, but I don't recall anything about a witness who needed to be interviewed. Of course, that's been years ago, so I'm not saying he didn't tell me or that he might have told the investigator, just that I don't recall it."

Judge Bradley Vance Thompson still had excellent antenna to detect the political winds. He wasn't about to let himself become embroiled in this controversy if he could help it.

*****

The following morning a meeting was convened in Paul Scarsdale's office. Southard and the district attorney listened as Remington related his conversation with Judge Thompson from the previous afternoon. As he finished, James Southard showed a hint of a smile that vanished instantly when Scarsdale threw the fountain pen he was holding across the room.

"That son of a bitch Thompson will use his selective memory to squirm his way out of any responsibility for this," Scarsdale exploded. "Sure he had me on the team to prosecute Jordan, but I was never involved in those meetings. I was just there to do the work, and it's pretty obvious now, to take the fall if he screwed something up."

James Southard smiled again. "You've got to hand it to Bradley Vance Thompson! He has the best political weathervane in Harris County."

"Well, the question we need to answer is what to do now. I can tell you that the beginning of every conversation I have with the media will be, *as you know this trial took place before I was elected District Attorney.* That SOB may think he doesn't have any liability here, but I'll make sure he does." Scarsdale's face was beet red as he spoke. "So update me on the status of the appeals."

"Boss, the first thing we should do is to anticipate a new appeal. It will be based on the information they discovered from our file. I think they have an excellent chance of getting a new trial. So that brings us to the other two appeals. The Court will be issuing its opinions any day now. If we are going to try to make a deal, it has to be expedited," Southard said.

Scarsdale looked from Southard to Remington. "What do you think Johnny? Should we sit on this and see what the court says on the other appeals or should we try to cut our losses?"

"I'm a little uncomfortable giving advice on the appeals, since James is the expert and they are his cases, but from a purely political perspective I think it's worth considering a deal. I would concentrate on the DNA testing. We could offer to test the sweater, but agree to no conditions regarding what happens after the tests are concluded.

"Even if Jordan's DNA is not on the sweater it doesn't automatically get him a new trial. If there is DNA from a third party, chances are we'll never know who that person is, or at least it won't be known for years, until after a substantial database has been built similar to what we have on fingerprints." Remington's analysis was quick and accurate.

"What do you think, James?" Paul Scarsdale wanted time to consider what he would do.

James Southard looked at Johnny Remington and smiled slightly again as he spoke. "Boss, Johnny here actually believes we are in the business of seeking justice, not judging our success by counting convictions. If you agree, then I think his suggestion is excellent. Even if you don't agree with him, there's good reason to proceed in the manner which he laid out, but just know that with the testing comes the possibility of surprise."

Scarsdale's face flushed as he said, "I'll tell you this! Remington doesn't have to face the voters every four years. I do! In this case justice has already been served by a jury. I'm not interested in revisiting justice, but I don't want this office embarrassed by sloppy work. Get Jefferson Clay in here as soon as you can. We'll give him his DNA tests, but no new trial, at least I hope not." With that, Paul Scarsdale picked up his phone as if to dismiss his visitors.

*****

When Jefferson Clay received the phone call from James Southard, he was walking out of his office to meet a client. The two agreed he would be at the district attorney's office after lunch. When he arrived, he was surprised to learn the meeting would be with Scarsdale, Remington and Southard. Usually very business-like, Clay decided this morning to begin the meeting with humor.

"So you guys finally talked to that witness who has been trying to give you information on the Jordan murder case for the last nine years; and you've called me down to apologize to my client, right?" Although he smiled at the three men sitting across the table, it was clear Paul Scarsdale wasn't interested in small talk.

"Clay, I've decided to agree to allow you to conduct DNA testing on the sweater if you think it's important to your client. Of course, we insist the testing be done at the FBI laboratory and that we receive the results simultaneously."

"Why would you agree to this just days before we are likely to get a decision from the court? You guys get your mail early and find out the ruling is in my favor?" Clay saw nothing but red flags in Scarsdale's proposal.

"We don't have any more information about the decision than you do. I am making this offer because in light of the information that my predecessor in this office apparently overlooked, interviewing a potential witness, I not only want to be fair, I want the total appearance of fairness. We're seeking justice here just as you are." Scarsdale was playing a weak poker hand.

"And what if my client's DNA is not found on the sweater?"

"It means nothing. You'll just do whatever you decide to do."

"And if a third party's DNA is found on the sweater?"

"Look, Clay, you are not getting any deals. Take it or leave it. If you get the best outcome from the DNA testing that you can imagine, you're still going to have to prove that it means something regarding the conviction of your client."

It had always been difficult for Paul Scarsdale to give ground in a legal argument and his actions revealed that he hadn't changed since becoming the district attorney.

Clay ignored his ranting and continued, "You know I intend to file a second motion for a new trial based on the evidence and witnesses who were not revealed to us before trial. Besides that, I may get a good call from the Court on the ineffective counsel argument.

"You are doing this because you know eventually there will be a new trial. When that happens, I'll get the DNA testing. But I don't care about your motivation. I'll have my staff contact you to make arrangements for the testing."

As the men stood, Scarsdale took one parting shot. "By the way, Clay, you know I am not intentionally trying to keep anybody who is innocent in prison, including your client. It's your job to prove he didn't commit the crime he was convicted of. I'd appreciate it if the next time you decide to talk to the media, you would consider being truthful about that."

Clay held out his hand to shake and as he did he responded, "Paul, you can bet your ass that I'm going to prove my client didn't commit the crime you convicted him of and if this office doesn't get with the program you're going to see more inflammatory remarks from me than you can imagine." He smiled as he turned and walked out of the office.

Justice Denied

Chapter Thirty Three

Bobby was beginning his tenth year behind bars. He had developed no real friendships during that time. The relationship with his cellmate, Delbert Matheson, was unusual for two reasons. First, it was uncommon for inmates to remain cellmates for a long period of time, but in this case both men had stayed out of trouble and kept the same jobs in the prison system, so they had given no reason for the warden to move them.

Even more unusual was that even though they had been in such close proximity for so long, they had never developed more than a cautious acceptance that they could survive as cellmates. Neither made any effort at friendship and, at the same time, had learned to negotiate quietly the issues that arise when two men are thrown together in such hostile circumstances.

Bobby appreciated the attitudes of Mr. Martin, the female guard, Officer Fleming and the teacher in his college program, Ms. Halliday, but none of them had ever lowered their defenses to allow him even a peek at their personal lives. He often fantasized that he was released from prison and met Ms. Halliday on the outside, even though he didn't even know if she was married. He knew she reminded him of Regina.

Notwithstanding the lack of personal relationships, Bobby trained himself not to allow his mind to wallow in depression. He became quite adept at practicing quiet meditation, even in the noisy environment of the prison system. He was known as a convict who wanted to be left alone.

After working at the license plate plant for nearly eight years, an older black inmate who had been at the Wynne Prison Unit for 25 years and now worked with him, found an opportunity to have a short conversation with Bobby. "You know they ain't never forgot about you, don't you?"

The comment surprised Bobby. "What are you talking about?" he asked.

"The Bloods, they ain't forgot what you did to Jigger." The inmate walked away before Bobby Jordan could ask another question.

After that short warning, he became even more isolated; always paying attention to make sure he stayed away from groups of black inmates. When he was in the law library, the cafeteria or a college class, he watched for any sign that another inmate might be studying him or making a habit of sitting at a desk close to him. When he saw no patterns and there had been no threatening incidents, he questioned whether the old inmate really knew anything about the Bloods, but he remained alert for any indication of such danger.

*****

When Jefferson Clay told Bobby that the district attorney had agreed to allow DNA tests to be performed on the Houston Oilers sweater, he was happy but reserved. Clay was surprised that he wasn't more enthusiastic after hearing the news.

"Mr. Clay, I've been here 10 years. My family is gone. I write a letter once a year to my son and never get a response. A few years ago, getting out of here was all that mattered. Today I'm not sure my life would be much different on the outside. Oh, I wouldn't have to worry as much about being attacked by some crazy inmate. I would appreciate being away from the noise and there would be no more strip searches, but I could never put my life back where it was that morning before I discovered Regina's body in our bedroom.

"So I'm happy the tests will be performed on the sweater and I hope someday my son will know that I didn't kill his mother. But to tell you the truth, I am at peace with my life.

"Don't get me wrong. I really appreciate what you are doing and if they ever open those doors and say *Bobby Jordan, you're a free man*, I'll move pretty fast to breathe that free air, but the peace I feel now won't change on the outside. You can't fix yesterday and you can't count on tomorrow, so I'm sorry I can't show the excitement you thought I would, but thanks."

Jefferson Clay left Huntsville that day as depressed as he could ever remember being. He had not learned the secrets of meditation and the practice of Zen that Bobby Jordan obviously enjoyed.

Chapter Thirty Four

The arrangements were made and to Jefferson Clay's great relief, the much discussed and debated Houston Oilers sweater which had been stored for so many years as evidence in the Regina Jordan murder case was located and submitted for testing. Now began another long wait.

While the actual testing of DNA can be done in a relatively short period of time, the criminal justice aspect of the testing slows the process to a great degree. The chain of custody of the evidence is important, as well as the scientific validity of the actual testing. Bureaucracy plays a part in slowing down the outcome as well. Four months after the sweater was submitted for testing, both the district attorney's office and Clay received the results.

Blood and hair samples taken from the sweater were tested. The results were that Regina Jordan's blood was found on the sweater, as well as another person's blood and strands of hair. Bobby Jordan's DNA was not. Several hair samples were tested and all tests indicated the hair belonged to an unknown male to whom the unidentified blood also matched.

Along with the notification of the results of the testing, both parties were notified that the samples would be submitted to the Combined DNA Index System (CODIS) - a computerized database of stored

DNA profiles that have been created by federal, state and local law enforcement crime laboratories. In 1994, Congress had authorized the FBI to operate the CODIS program. Again, because of backlogged requests for such information, the wait was expected to be months.

*****

On the same day the notification was received regarding the DNA tests, both Clay and the district attorney received the remaining opinions from the Texas Court of Criminal Appeals. The appeals of the defendant, Robert Jordan, were denied in both cases.

The earlier decision made by the district attorney to agree with the defense and move forward with the DNA tests now caused considerable debate and second-guessing. After several days of this internal debate, D.A. Paul Scarsdale issued an edict in a meeting of all his chief prosecutors.

"I know everyone has been beating a dead horse over the Jordan case. Some believe if we had only waited a little longer the court would have settled the DNA issue in our favor. That's not true! If we had not agreed to the testing, Jefferson Clay would have likely appealed to the U.S. Supreme Court on several issues. So I suggest you each get your staff back to work on your assigned caseloads and let me worry about whether the right decision was made on this case."

*****

Two months later, a call from an old friend in the FBI Washington, D.C. office caused Paul Scarsdale to begin second guessing the decision himself.

"Paul, this is Dennis Sadler. I'm calling to give you a heads up. You guys submitted a DNA analysis request on a Regina Jordan murder case. Are you familiar with the case?"

"I sure am, Dennis. It's one of those cases that just won't go away. What's up?"

"Well, your office and the defense lawyer will be getting notification that we have matched one of the DNA samples to another murder case in Houston. We still don't have a match to any person in our database because that case is still unsolved, but in 1991, Jo Anne Scanlon was murdered in Houston and the DNA on the sweater matches that taken from the scene of the Scanlon murder. I figure this might be a little public relations problem for you, so I wanted to give you advance notice."

"No doubt about it being a problem. Are you telling me there is no match to a suspect?"

"No, no, Paul. Our system allows us to run comparisons in several ways. It's being run now against our database of persons who's DNA we have obtained. Any results should be in by the end of the day."

"Thanks, Dennis. I appreciate the call. We'll talk soon. I've got to get my staff on this right away."

Thirty minutes later, Remington and Southard were meeting with the district attorney after being advised of the information received from Sadler.

"I got the file on Jo Anne Scanlon. There are a lot of similarities to the Jordan murder case." Remington looked at both men before continuing, "It was an early morning murder. She was beaten pretty severely with one arm broken. No sign of forced entry into the house, although an acquaintance told the investigators that Scanlon never locked her doors."

"So we need to get out in front of this," Scarsdale interrupted. "The question is, should we bring Clay in on it or just make the announcement ourselves. You know he didn't mind blindsiding us in the newspaper with that witness...what was his name...Baldwin wasn't it?"

Remington sat forward in his chair. "You know it doesn't really make any difference at this point. We're going to have to get Bobby Jordan released. In light of this information, I'm a little sick of worrying about political fallout. Jordan's been in prison for nearly eleven years."

Paul Scarsdale stared at Johnny Remington as if Remington had just accused him of a heinous crime, but his response was more subtle than either of his employees expected.

"You are right, Johnny. This is about moving forward as quickly as we can to see that justice is served. Call Clay. Get him over here and let's make it public that we are correcting an injustice. You agree James?"

"It's probably the smart thing to do." James Southard didn't care to comment further.

That afternoon, after discussing the new information with Jefferson Clay, Scarsdale simply released a media advisory that due to new information in the Regina Jordan murder case, he and Bobby Jordan's attorney would ask a judge to set aside the murder conviction. Both Clay and Scarsdale spent most of the next day talking with various media representatives about the case.

*****

The informal flow of information in Texas prisons is much the same as it is with any group of people who spend long periods of time in close proximity. The morning after the Harris County District Attorney's office issued the news release that a judge would be asked to set aside Bobby Jordan's conviction, the news had spread throughout the Wynne Unit. However, Bobby had decided to lay-in that morning and miss the trip to the cafeteria for breakfast where he would have undoubtedly heard about his good fortune.

So it was that when he was escorted to work at the license plate plant, he still didn't know that he was soon to be a free man. As he proceeded through the counting procedures before admission to his work area, Officer Fleming spoke to him.

"Congratulations, Jordan"

"I'm sorry officer, what did you say?"

"I said congratulations," Fleming responded more loudly. "Looks like you'll be leaving us soon."

She could tell be the expression on Jordan's face that he had not yet heard of his good fortune. Fleming also knew that she couldn't hold up the inmate count to explain it to him.

"Jordan, talk to Mr. Martin when you get in the plant. He'll explain."

As Bobby Jordan walked to his assignment, Mr. Martin approached him. "Jordan, I'm happy for you. Congratulations."

"Mr. Martin, I just heard the same thing from Officer Fleming. I have no idea what you are talking about."

Martin explained that an article in the morning edition of the Chronicle reported his conviction would be set aside. He wished Bobby good luck and told him he wished the release was immediate, but it probably would be weeks, if not months, before it was official.

As he settled into the routine of placing license plates in boxes to be shipped, Bobby thought about the news. If he was really going to be getting out, he would need to be ever more cautious about his surroundings in the weeks to come. If Jigger's friends knew he was going to be released, they were likely to make their move to settle the score for Jigger.

Chapter Thirty Five

Two days after learning that he would soon be free, Bobby received a visit from Jefferson Clay and John Cooksey. Cooksey had asked Clay if he would object to him making the trip to discuss Bobby's release. Now that the appeal had been denied alleging ineffective counsel and the defense team had no reason to take the issue to a higher court, Cooksey felt compelled to be there to celebrate with his former client.

Once seated across the grey metal table from him, Jefferson Clay advised Bobby there would be a hearing the following day during which the judge was expected to sign the order setting aside Bobby's conviction. Since tomorrow was a Friday, Clay doubted Bobby's release would occur before the next Monday.

The lawyers were in a festive mood, but when Bobby was told that he would not be released until the following week his expression couldn't mask the worry.

"Is there any way to speed this up and get me out tomorrow?" Bobby directed the question to Clay.

"Bobby, it's been eleven years. One more weekend shouldn't be that tough." Clay didn't understand.

Bobby Jordan's lips were trembling as he began to speak. "Mr. Cooksey, do you remember the problem

I had with the black convict right after I got here? The guy named Jigger?"

"I do, Bobby, but I thought that was settled years ago. At any rate, you'll be out by Monday, Tuesday at the latest." John Cooksey looked at Clay as if for confirmation and Clay nodded in the affirmative.

"I was told just a few weeks ago that Jigger's friends haven't forgotten. The news of my release was out before I knew about it. I'm worried they will try to move on me before I can be released." Bobby bit his lower lip as he told the two lawyers of his concern.

"We'll talk to the warden before we leave." Jefferson Clay stood as did Cooksey. "We'll make sure he knows of the threat."

*****

The two men left and Bobby was returned to his cell. The meeting with his lawyers had ended in time for Bobby to enter his cell just before his cellblock was turned out for dinner. Minutes later, he heard the familiar call as the cell door rolled open.

"Cellblock B2, Chow time."

Bobby and Delbert Matheson were herded with the other inmates on their cellblock to the Day Room to await the trip to the cafeteria. As Bobby entered the Day Room, a surge of several inmates toward the door engulfed him. He felt the deep penetration of the blade immediately. It was shoved in an upward motion under his left ribcage hard and fast. He looked into the vacant stare of a white inmate who then tried to plunge the blade deeper before releasing the weapon and fading back into the crowd of inmates. Bobby slumped to the floor.

As he came to rest on the concrete floor, the sea of humanity around him instinctively retreated from his body. Delbert Matheson screamed for a guard and knelt over Bobby as he tried to find a pulse. Minutes later a gurney was rolled into the Day Room and Bobby was loaded on it and moved out to the infirmary. His cellmate, Delbert Matheson, who had never wanted to become close to any other inmate, including Bobby Jordan, placed his face in his hands and cried as he knelt on his knees.

Jefferson Clay and John Cooksey drove out the driveway of the visitor's parking lot and soon turned left onto the service road to enter the freeway. They were on their way home after being assured by the warden that the prison system was well aware their client would be released in a matter of days and that his safety was a high priority. The warden told them he would have the staff pay particular attention to Jordan's safety and would place him in isolation if deemed necessary. None of the three were aware that it was too late for such precautions.

*****

On Friday morning at ten a.m., a hearing was held during which the judge agreed to set aside the conviction of Bobby Jordan. The paperwork to set him free began its slow movement through the government spider web of bureaucracy where it would eventually reach the desk of the Wynne Prison Unit warden some time the following week.

The attorneys were bombarded with questions as they exited the courthouse. When would Jordan be released and would he be available for questions? Was the investigation to be reopened? If Jordan wasn't the murderer, could it be assumed the real murderer had been stalking the streets of Houston for the last eleven years?

After nearly an hour, Jefferson Clay returned to his office only to be told as he entered that Paul Scarsdale was holding on line one. "Jefferson, have you been in contact with the prison system this morning?"

"No. Why would I? We can't do anything for Bobby until the judge's orders are in the hands of the warden."

"I'm afraid you won't be able to do anything for your client even then, Jefferson. He was stabbed by another inmate late yesterday. He didn't make it. I'm sorry."

Clay was too stunned to respond. Hadn't the warden assured him Bobby's safety was a priority? How could this happen?

"I'm sorry, Paul. I need to hang up the phone. I can't talk to you now."

After phone calls to John Cooksey and Jack Whittington, Jefferson Clay sat staring out his office window for an hour before leaving the office. He didn't return until Thursday of the following week.

Chapter Thirty Six

On Monday morning following the death of Bobby Jordan, Harris County District Attorney Paul Scarsdale asked his secretary to check with the F.B.I. office regarding the DNA sample from the unknown suspect in the Jordan and Scanlon murder cases. It had occurred to him over the weekend that he had not received a report regarding whether the evidence taken from these two crime scenes were matched with a named suspect.

Within the hour, the secretary reported there was a hit on the suspect and the reason for the slow response was because the suspect's DNA information was not been in the national database, CODIS, but had been matched with the State of California database. While California shares its DNA information with the F.B.I., in this case the information had yet to be sent to the CODIS system. In an abundance of caution, the analyst who ran the check and got no match in the CODIS system decided to run it independently in three state database systems he knew were overburdened with the collecting, categorizing and submission of such information to the federal government.

The result was that the California system matched the evidence with Bradford Stark, who had been arrested in Los Angeles for the attempted rape and murder of a young housewife just five weeks earlier. Unlike the Houston cases, the Los Angeles victim heard Stark slide the patio door open and ran to the bedroom where her husband kept an old army model .45 automatic for home protection.

As she attempted to retrieve the weapon from the nightstand beside the bed, Stark struck her behind the ear. As she fell, he ripped most of her blouse from her body, but his luck had run out. She latched her fingers firmly around the grip of the .45 and began firing. Hit in the leg, Bradford Stark limped from the home and was arrested a few minutes later when police were responding to a call from neighbors who heard the gun shots.

Several months later, Bradford Stark was extradited to Texas to face murder charges in the two Houston cases. After the Court appointed an attorney for Stark, a deal was struck. Stark confessed to the two murders and in return Paul Scarsdale did not seek the death penalty. Bradford Stark was sentenced to two life sentences.

In his confession, Stark admitted he had first spotted Regina Jordan in her back yard while painting a house on the street behind the Jordan home. This occurred about two weeks before the murder. Stark stated that he spent the entire week watching Bobby Jordan leave each morning at about the same time. He also noted that Regina appeared to sleep in after her husband left for work, usually appearing in the back yard with a cup of coffee at least an hour after her husband was gone.

During the four days that he observed the activity at the Jordan home, he never saw B.J. and didn't know the Jordan family included a child. It was later determined by talking to the neighbor whose house Stark painted and obtaining the dates he was on the job, that those dates matched a ten day period when Regina's parents took B.J. with them on a vacation to West Texas.

On the morning of the murder, Bradford Stark stood at the corner of the Jordan home as Bobby backed his truck from the garage. As he closed the garage door with his remote and drove away, Stark quickly rounded the corner and entered the garage. He had been concerned Bobby would see the garage door stop rolling to a close, but Bobby never looked back. The door from the garage to the house was never locked.

When Stark entered the Jordan home he proceeded to the kitchen and found the knife. He then located the bedroom where he had anticipated that Regina Jordan would still be asleep. Instead she was standing beside the bed and had started to slip a pair of panties over her left foot. She began to scream and he attacked her. His statement read:

She started fighting like a man and I had to knock her down, but she was right back up and I twisted her arm until I knew it was broken. I hit her again and she was dazed. That's when I cut her throat. I wanted her even though she was dead. I pulled my sweater off and was getting ready to drop my jeans when a kid opened the door. I couldn't kill a kid so I ran. When I got to my car I left and never went back to that neighborhood.

When asked if he had any remorse for the murder or for the fact that Bobby Jordan was sent to prison for a crime he committed, Stark replied simply, *a man's gotta do what a man's gotta do.*

Chapter Thirty Seven

When B.J. Jordan was sixteen years old, Jefferson Clay arranged a meeting approved by his grandparents, the Whites. The meeting included Clay, John Cooksey, and Bob Martin, who had supervised Bobby Jordan the entire time he was at the Wynne prison unit, Bobby's sister and brother-in-law, Linda and Jack Seneca, Bobby's brother Dale, and Mr. and Mrs. White. The purpose of the meeting was to let B.J. know more about the father he had spent so little time with.

As a child, he didn't understand why he had to endure a two hour road trip to Huntsville and visit with a man he barely remembered. After his father was murdered in prison when B.J. was 13 years old, he began asking questions about Bobby, his mother, and the circumstances that caused his father to be in prison. Although the Whites answered the questions as well as they could, they were not experts at dealing with such emotional issues.

Eventually they engaged a psychologist who worked with B.J. on a number of issues, including his guilt for having rejected his father at an early age. The meeting Clay arranged was a result of his conversation with the psychologist who thought it would be good for B.J. to hear about Bobby from some of the people who had been close to him during the last years of his life. The meeting was held in the psychologist's office.

It was an interesting meeting, as described by the psychologist, because each of the attendees was given an opportunity to tell B.J. something about his dad. Not a single one tried to make Bobby into a hero. As Jefferson Clay said, Bobby was just 'every man' who wanted a good life for his child and a happy home.

Linda Seneca cried when she described growing up with her brother. Dale Jordan told funny stories about their childhood. Jenny White asked B.J. to forgive her for not having encouraged him to continue visiting his father in prison and told him of the good things Bobby did for B.J.'s mother. Robert White simply told the boy his dad was a good man who society had failed, but that B.J.'s responsibility was to move on with his life. He said Bobby would not want B.J.'s life defined by the incident that had brought them all together this day.

Bob Martin didn't talk long, but he said Bobby Jordan was the most unusual convict he ever had contact with during more than fifteen years of working in the prison system. He said he always believed Bobby was innocent because of the manner in which he conducted himself. He was a man who refused to be drawn into the vicious culture of prison life and that was apparent to those who came into contact with him on a daily basis.

When John Cooksey stood to speak, he simply asked B.J. to remember his father as a man willing to give up freedom rather than to lose his honor. He said he regretted he had not been successful in keeping Bobby out of prison.

Finally Jefferson Clay spoke of Bobby. He strove to bring the meaning of all the speeches together.

"Bobby, you are only sixteen years old and your life is ahead of you. Your father loved you. Forgive those you believe harmed your father, and, as a result, you. Take to heart what your grandfather told you. Don't let this incident become the defining moment of your life. I understand you have all the excuses anyone would ever need to reject the great American dream. But you, like the rest of us who knew Bobby Jordan, have a duty to rise above the bitterness of life and the anger at those who fail us and to try to change the parts of society that did this to your dad."

With those final words, the meeting was over.

Chapter Thirty Eight

On January 19, 2010, standing before a room filled with one-hundred-fifty police officers and attorneys representing police departments and prosecutors' offices from throughout the State of Texas, the speaker began.

"Good morning ladies and gentlemen. My name is Bobby Jordan and I am here today to discuss with you an issue some will be uncomfortable with. It is, however, an issue each of you should take very seriously if you are committed to serving the citizens of your community and of this great State of Texas. How many of you have heard of the Regina Jordan murder case?" Several hands were raised throughout the room.

"Regina Jordan was my mother. My father, whose name I proudly share, was Bobby Jordan. I lost them both due to a tragic miscarriage of justice that was perpetrated when my father was wrongly convicted of killing my mother. Eleven years later a judge set aside that conviction. However, just hours before the judge rendered his decision and three days before my father would have been released from prison, he was murdered by another inmate. There was no opportunity to rectify the mistakes of the criminal justice system for my father.

"This miscarriage of justice was not entirely the fault of one or more prosecutors or police officers, although I will tell the story of some of those who were involved in my father's case and how they contributed to the failure to seek justice. Instead, the tragedy of Bobby Jordan, Sr. was perpetrated by a flawed system, a system that rewards prosecutors and police officers for the number of criminal cases cleared and the number of persons that are sent to prison, but which exacts no measurement, penalty nor reward for how well or if, indeed, justice is served at all in these cases.

"Now, when I asked how many of you knew of the Regina Jordan murder case, roughly ten hands went up. That's understandable since the murder occurred more than twenty years ago and most of you were not involved in the criminal justice system at the time; in fact, as I look around the room, I am convinced that some of you were not even born then. So, how many of you are aware of the case of the disbarment of Judge Bradley Vance Thompson?"

This time all of the attorneys and most of the police officers raised their hands. "Does anyone know why he was removed from the bench and disbarred from practicing law in Texas?"

A young prosecutor in the back of the room stood and proclaimed that Thompson was disbarred for perjury in both a deposition and before a grand jury.

"You are correct, sir, and I might add that Judge Thompson, who was the district attorney at the time of my mother's murder, is the only person involved in the investigation and prosecution of the death of Regina Jordan who suffered any formal discipline or rebuke for that miscarriage of justice.

"Let me tell you about the cast of characters who played a part in sending my father to prison where he met his death. By the way, I too carry the burden of having made bad decisions regarding my father's life. Although I was only two years old when my mother was murdered and thirteen when my father was murdered, I had rejected my father and hadn't seen him in more than five years. He sent me letters at least once each year to which I never responded.

"You see, I believed in the criminal justice system. I admired police officers and trusted the court system. My view was that he must have killed my mother, because the police and the courts wouldn't have sent him to prison otherwise. How wrong I was!

"Judge Thompson was, by all accounts, a good prosecutor. But when information that might have been helpful to my father's defense came to light during the investigation, he decided to hide it from the defense attorney. He made it about WINNING, not about justice.

"Thompson's prosecuting team included Paul Scarsdale. Paul was a good lawyer also, but he spent several years fighting the efforts of defense lawyers to have DNA testing done on the evidence which later caused a judge to set aside my father's conviction. He made it about WINNING, not about justice.

"Johnny Remington was a young, inexperienced prosecutor at the time of the trial, and by his own account, raised questions about the case then, as well as years later, when Scarsdale was fighting efforts to test the evidence.

"I've come to know Johnny quite well in the years since my father's death and he serves on the board of directors of Seeking Justice, Inc.; the organization I created to change the mindset of those who toil daily in the criminal justice system. We want a new paradigm in which the rewards go to those who dispense justice and not just those with high clearance and conviction rates. With that said, I believe Johnny should have been even more assertive when he recognized his bosses were about keeping scorecards rather than about dispensing justice.

"There were three primary investigators from the police department who worked on my mother's murder case.

"The lead detective or, maybe more accurately, the dominant one, was a man named Jimmy Starbuck. He is long since retired from the police department. When I attempted to discuss this case with him a couple of years ago, he refused to have a conversation with me. I've had discussions with a number of people who knew Detective Starbuck. Some of the words used to describe him were relentless, egotistical, hot dog, know-it-all, and professional. My conclusion is the same as it is for Scarsdale and Thompson. Jimmy Starbuck made it about WINNING, not about justice!

"Marcus Wilson was also assigned to work on the Jordan case. His was a sad story. Wilson retired the year after my father's conviction and died of cirrhosis of the liver the year after my father was murdered in prison. He wrote a letter addressed to me. He had his wife mail it to me upon his death. Those who knew him prior to his retirement say he was burned out as a detective. He was cynical, even by police officer standards.

"In his letter he apologized to me. By the way, he was the only person involved in this case to ever do that. He said in the letter he should have retired long before he did, because his efforts as a detective had become how to avoid work, not to solve crimes. He told me he should have done a better job when working on my father's case. He said he was tormented by the case once it was learned the real murderer and the evidence that ultimately proved who the murderer was, were both hiding in plain sight.

"I visited with his wife who told me he thought when he retired he would golf and fish to fill his days of retirement, but was surprised when, after less than a year, he was bored with both. She also believed he missed the respect he enjoyed as a police officer. He once told her that after he retired he was just another old man in the neighborhood.

"Marcus Wilson wasn't in it to win and he wasn't in it to seek justice. Sadly, Marcus Wilson had checked out long before he retired. I think he recognized that about himself when he learned my father was murdered and that's why he wrote the letter.

"T.J. Lawson worked with Starbuck and Wilson on the case. He was young and idealistic. It was clear, when the defense finally got the opportunity to look at his notes, that T.J. was appalled at the manner in which the investigation of my father was conducted. There is no doubt he raised questions to his lieutenant and the senior detectives, but he stopped there.

"The attorneys who took the case to attempt to have my father set free all believe that T.J. Lawson intentionally pointed them in the direction of looking at his notes. That may seem to be of little importance, but it was enough. Sometimes just doing what is right, even if it seems insignificant at the time, can make the difference. By the way, T.J. is also serving on the board of my non-profit organization and he still has some of that idealism he had when the Jordan murder case came his way.

"That finishes my review of the case. After lunch we will continue with where we go from here."

As the group broke for lunch, B.J. looked for T.J. Lawson and Johnny Remington. He would introduce them to the group during the afternoon session.

*****

After lunch the classroom was filled again. Both Remington and Lawson stood beside B.J. as he introduced them.

"In a few minutes these two gentlemen will talk to you about their experiences and about different methods of evaluating the work of prosecutors and police investigators. So I'll just finish with this.

"Had it not been for an organization named The Innocence Project and two local lawyers, John Cooksey and Jefferson Clay, my father's name would likely never have been cleared. My mission through Seeking Justice is to attempt to make efforts like theirs unnecessary or, at least, very rare in the future.

"The Innocence Project has been instrumental in helping untold numbers of persons who were wrongly convicted. Mr. Clay and Cooksey chose to stick with my father's case even after there was no funding for the appeals. In fact, both of these gentlemen and The Innocence Project spent hundreds of thousands of dollars in time, as well as cash to pursue my father's case.

"But the question for all of us is: *How do we change a system so that efforts such as theirs are rarely necessary in our society?*

"Neither I nor my colleagues have all the answers, but before I leave, let me suggest two things for you to consider.

"First, if you are burned out as a prosecutor or a detective, leave the profession. If there are reasons you feel you can't leave, ask for a position in the criminal justice system not involved in making critical decisions about the lives of others.

"The other thought I would leave you with is that if you still have some of the idealism and desire to do it right, don't be cowered by colleagues who have bought into a system that condones shoddy investigative techniques or short-cuts to prosecutions.

"If you will do these things and if we can change the grading system for the jobs you do, maybe there will be justice for my father and others like him. Thank you!"

Also by Larry Watts

The Missing Piece
The Park Place Rangers (A book of short-stories)
Homicide in Black and White
Rich Man, Dead Man
Murder on the Seawall

About the Author

Larry Watts worked for more than twenty years as a patrol officer and police investigator in Houston, Texas. He then spent another twenty years working for an organization representing police officers throughout the State of Texas. During his over forty years of work with the criminal justice system he has experienced the victories and the shortcomings of that system first-hand. Watts' first novel, *The Missing Piece,* has been acclaimed in the law enforcement community as the writing of a seasoned professional who keeps the reader enthralled with the story he tells.

Watts is a graduate of Antioch University where he received a Bachelor of Arts Degree in Labor Studies and of Harvard Trade Union Program at Harvard University's School of Business. He resides in the Gulf Coast area of Texas with his wife, Carolyn.

You can read more about Larry at his website, WWW.LarryWatts.net and he encourages readers to e-mail him with your thoughts about his writing at Larry@LarryWatts.Net.

www.ingramcontent.com/pod-product-compliance
Lightning Source LLC
Chambersburg PA
CBHW070922180626
46817CB00003B/1166